GW01162015

The Courtship of Nocker Yates

by

Robert Brown

First published 1989 by Countyvise Limited, 1 & 3 Grove Road, Rock Ferry, Birkenhead, Wirral, Merseyside L42 3XS.

Copyright © Robert Brown, 1989.

Photoset and printed by Birkenhead Press Limited, 1 & 3 Grove Road, Rock Ferry, Birkenhead, Merseyside L42 3XS.

ISBN 0 907768 34 2.

All rights reserved. No part of this publication may be reproduced, stored in a retrieval system, or transmitted, in any form, or by any means, electronic, chemical, mechanical, photocopying, recording or otherwise, without the prior permission of the publisher.

GLOSSARY

(Or in other words explanations of what Scouse words mean)

Made up ....Pleased, delighted
Bevvied... Drunk
Having a bevvy ....Having a drink
Under the arm ....Rotten, lousy
Blocker Man... Boss

N.B.
There is no dirty book shop behind Cazneau Street (alas) which is pronounced by all the best Scousers as Kaznew Street. The street itself has almost disappeared into the Mersey Tunnel approach, eheu fugaces.

The two little judies Satu and Sanna live next door to me by the way. Their parents have read the stories and will not be doing me for libel — so they say!

1

"Change never does no-one no good," says me Mam, and she could be right at that. Take me and Nocker Yates for instance.

There was a time when we was mates, sharing life's joys and sorrows, and going to see Everton play at home, regular. We also have a nice little car-minding business too. Fifty pee to see that nobody sprays paint all over the Rolls, while youse is in the alehouse with the lady, Mister — that sort of thing.

Then Basher, who is our beloved headmaster, leaves to go some place else. Word gets round that a certain A. Hitler, who is not dead as is supposed, has signed him up to teach his Gestapo a thing or two, seeing as how this same Basher will chop the hand off of you with his stick just for breathing too loud.

Be that as it may, we are all dead chuffed when we see the seat of his keks going through the door. Next, naturally, we get to asking ourselves what the new blocker man is going to be like. So when Duff Riley comes in one morning and says his cousin knows about him, we are all ears.

"He's from one of them experimental schools," says Duff who can use big words, "And he goes in for Free Expression."

"What the friggin hell's that?" says Nocker.

"It means no work, and have a quiet ciggy in the bog whenever you feel like," Duff says back.

Of course we all say three cheers to this; and soon after the queer feller himself clocks in and hangs up his hat in the headmaster's room.

Everything is magic at first, it all happens just like what Duff says. The lads don't do no work and nobody minds when you smoke in the lavvy. But then this new blocker man starts making changes.

First they get girls in. This means we lose two footie periods and have to do something called Modern Educational Dance instead. We all moan like the clappers when they make us ponce round the hall with the judies and we get splinters in our bare feet.

Next they start having something what they call Optional Subjects. Everyone in 4D is told they can either do Remedial English or Sex Education.

"I'm going to have a bash at Sex," Nocker tells me.

"What for?" I ask him.

"For the sake of all them little Nockers yet unborn, what mightn't show up otherwise," he says, "and for a laugh".

"Stick to Remedial English like your father and grandfather before you," I tell him back. "That stuff won't do you no good, you dirty old man."

And it turns out I am right in the end at that.

For the next few days I don't see much of him. Then I hear a rumour going about the place that he is courting! Naturally I am most interested to find out more, so I keep a look out for him, special, and when I see him in the school yard I go up to have a word. Just as I get close I see some judy is nattering to him. She clears off quick when I get there, but not before I get to noticing her face, which is like the back end of a bus what has been carrying some Man. United supporters after they lose four-nil to Everton.

I ask him is that the lady I hear all the lads talking about, and he says, yes it is, and that love has come into his life at last. But he has a kind of funny look on him as he says it, which gets me to thinking a bit.

"Look," I say back to him, "I don't believe all this love and kisses malarkey, you can just pull the other leg what has got bells on. I think youse is up to something. So tell us all about it, we're mates aren't we?"

"Scouse," he says, "don't spread this around to nobody, but I think I am on to a real good thing." Then he tells me the tale as follows.

It seems that Nocker goes to his first Sex lesson and is feeling very cheesed, because they don't tell him no dirty stuff, but keep going on all the time about something called an Amoeba. So he is just sitting there carving 'Everton Is Ace' on the desk, when someone sticks their nut round the classroom door and says everybody has got to go and see nurse immediate.

Nocker goes along with the rest, and after she combs out his hair looking for biddies, the nurse tells him to hang about while she does the girls, and then collect a note to take to hospital about his wonky sinus. So he is standing outside the medical room like a spare part at a wedding, when he hears such a racket going on inside he nearly swallows his chewy with shock. Next thing all the judies come busting out of the door, and these are screaming and fainting all over the place. They belt up the corridor like bats out of hell with the nurse judy close behind them — also going like the clappers. Last of all to come out is a cross-eyed girl who goes off, very slow, on her own.

Nocker is curious, naturally, and starts making enquiries. He learns that the cross-eyed tart is called Maggie, and it is her what is later to become his future beloved. It seems she has got something of a personal hygiene problem, but this only shows when she exerts herself and gets too hot. Up to now nobody gets to know about it as the fastest she shifts her fat bum is half of an mph, even when she is doing PE.

When the nurse tests her flat feet though, by asking her to hop about a bit the news gets round the place pretty smartish. In fact the pong is so fierce that even the nurse judy, what is used to such things, can't stand it. In fact she packs in being Florence Nightingale immediate and gets one of those jobs selling perfume door to door, to help her forget.

When Nocker hears all this and finds out as well that Maggie supports the Blues, he gets an idea. He starts off by chatting her up a bit, next he takes her to Saturday's match at Goodison. Soon as they get to the ground he says to the feller on the turnstile —

"Look here Mister, we lost our tickets. Let us in will youse?"

Naturally the turnstile feller has heard this one before and he tells Nocker to shove smartish, or he will batter him. So Nocker tells Maggie to start jumping up and down a bit, which she does. She begins to niff so bad that it makes our outside lavvy, what the landlord won't do nothing about, pong like Chanel No. 5.

All the queue what are waiting behind Nocker get the message immediate. They shoot back across the road a hundred yards at least and the turnstile feller is so scared everyone will go and watch Liverpool instead, what are playing at home too, that he lets Nocker and Maggie in for free and sticks them in the best spec, right next to the directors' box. Nocker is highly chuffed about this and Maggie is made up likewise; as she don't know his nose packed it in years ago and he can't smell a thing. She thinks he loves her for her intellect.

"So now," Nocker tells me, "I go all over the place for nothing. We even get to see the big game with Wolves last week and we travel first class too. I just get Maggie to run up and down the corridor a bit and the ticket inspector don't want to know. The buffet car feller gives us pies and coke to go away as well!"

Soon as Nocker finishes his tale I ask him, "How's about letting *me* in on the racket?"

"No — three's a crowd," he tells me. Also he says he has invested quite considerable in Maggie already, what with Mars bars and crisps and all the flowers he knocks off in the cemetery every day. So in the end we start having a nark and I walk away and leave him. We don't speak to one another no more.

But it don't last long this racket of Nocker's. In fact it packs in just after we have our barney. First of all, it seems when Maggie and him catch a train to watch Man. United play, they cop for a ticket collector what does his national service with the Catering Corps in Africa. This feller knows enough to creep up on Maggie — up-wind or something, and he gets so close he manages to get her name and address from her. The screwy ta-ta gives him the right one, so now the scuffers have got on to Nocker. They keep going round to his house, saying they will do him for swindling British Rail and each time this happens he gets a battering from his old feller.

Next thing it seems the last thing the nurse judy does before she goes off to be 'Your Avon Lady Calling' is to put Nocker down for an op. at the Ear, Nose and Throat. He comes out of the hozzy, three weeks before the Cup Final what he has been looking forward to seeing something rotten. But now his nose is as good as new and he can't stand Maggie near him to work the racket like he used to.

She don't understand this though, and keeps running after him asking why he don't love her no more. This makes him suffer considerable, but I say serve him right for busting up a real beautiful friendship and putting the mockers on the best little car-minding business this side of London Road.

As me Mam says though, "Life's Like That."

We're only here to save cemetery space really, according to my old lady.

2

Nocker Yates Goes to the Sales

"Starting the New Year," says me Mam, "is like watching a Scotsman standing on his head in a kilt — from the back. You know what's behind, but you've got no idea yet what it's like in front."

She tells you this every Jan. the First. But when me and me best mate Nocker Yates ask her what she's on about, she just shoves her hat on and pushes off down town to the sales with Nocker's old lady. They spend the whole day pushing and shoving with a million other judies and come back looking like they bumped into a mob of Man. United supporters after their team loses seven-nothing. Even so, they are made up even if they only manage to grab hold of half of a pair of torn knickers.

Me and Nocker try not to be around during these times. Otherwise they get hold of you and make you carry parcels. This means also, that you will most likely be shoved down the escalator at Marks and Sparks, and get your spare parts trod into the carpet at the bottom. This is very painful indeed, and no good at all for a growing lad.

This year though we come real unstuck, both of us. The old lady comes busting in me bedroom on the First of Jan, at eight a.m. — punctual to the minute. She says to me that I am to shift me fat bum, as she wants me to do a spot of fetching and carrying at the British Home Stores, Lewis's and suchlike.

"Ar eh Mam, how about asking me Da for a change?" I say.

But she says not to be a divvy, as don't I know the old feller will be celebrating New Year's Day as always, with his head stuck half way down the lavvy pan, spewing his ring up. Then she tips me out of bed and tells me to shove me keks on, smartish-like.

Ten minutes later we are both going down Scotty Road like the clappers, making for the bus stop by St. Anthony's Church. We find Nocker's old lady waiting for the bus when we get there, and a hundred other judies beside. Nocker is with her as well, leaning against the church railings, and looking like he is going to his own funeral.

Then the 85 comes along and there is a dirty big rush for it. Me and Nocker try to do a sneak upstairs, so as we can have a quiet ciggy, but they grab hold of us and tell us to stay down and be good boys.

This is very cheesing as we have got to stand all the way. Also we get stuck next to some tart what keeps going on at her boy friend all the time about getting married, and why doesn't he want to, just yet. Me and Nocker think that only a tart would ask a divvy question like that; it's like saying to a feller in Walton Jail,

"Why don't youse want to be hung tomorrer morning?"

But then Nocker finds some chewy in his pocket and this helps to pass the time a bit.

Soon as we get off the bus, our old ladies head for C & A's. They make for the dress department, and the next thing me and Nocker find ourselves loaded down with tons of frocks, what they are going to try on. Then we get told to go and wait for them by the changing rooms while they go look for a few dozen more.

So there we are, looking like a couple of spare parts at a wedding, hoping Duff Riley and none of the other lads don't come along and see us just now. Also, Nocker finds his chewy is losing its flavour, and he has to park it on the door-post of one of the changing rooms to get shut of it. So, what with one thing and the other, we are cheesed right up to the eyeballs.

Just then who shows up but the judy we see on the bus, none other. She has still got her boy friend with her and is yakking at him harder than ever about getting married. But he keeps his gob tight shut and don't answer nothing; as it is obvious he is making no statements without his lawyer with him. Next thing she tells him to wait and goes into the changing room to try something on.

In a minute she comes out again, wearing some kind of frilly dressing gown thing.

She says to her feller, "How about this for the honeymoon like?" but he still won't talk.

So, she starts twisting and poncing around a bit, as she thinks this will turn him on. Then, sudden-like, the end of the dressing gown sticks to Nocker's chewy what's still on the door-post and it falls right off of her onto the floor.

Me and Nocker are most embarrased when we see this, as she has took her frock off before she starts trying things on. This wouldn't matter so much, if she wasn't one of them tarts what go around bra-less. Just now she looks like the pictures in the dirty book shop behind Cazneau Street, where the lads all go for a free read and a cheap thrill.

But the boy friend is real made up, as it seems he never sees the goods when they are unwrapped before.

He says, "I *will* marry you Sharon, any time you like."

Naturally you might think the judy would be all chuffed about this, but she isn't, not one little bit. Straightaway she swipes him one across the gob with the back of her hand, and says,

"So, that's all *you* think about Terry Muldoon! I wouldn't marry the likes of youse, not if you was the last feller left alive on this earth!"

She goes and gets herself dressed and when she comes out again, she gives him another clout — on the lughole this time. Then she pushes off leaving him standing there.

Me and Nocker enjoy all this carry-on very much, as we think things are getting a lot less boring. But the feller sees us grinning and he gets a proper cob on. He comes on over to us and starts asking what we both think we are laughing at.

Of course we say back, "Nothing Mister," but that don't do no good. It begins to look like he is going to get cracking knocking our blocks off any minute now, so we decide the time has come to split — immediate.

We take off like the clappers and the feller comes on after us. He can run real fast too, and things is looking serious when Nocker spots this door.

"In 'ere Scouse!" he shouts me. We both duck through and bolt the door behind us. We hear banging from the other side, also a load of shouting and yelling. Then after a bit things go all quiet again.

While we are getting our breath back, I start to notice a funny pong, a bit like the make-up stuff like the tarts put on their faces. I mention this to Nocker and say I think this place niffs like a ladies' bog.

He takes a quick look round. Then he tells me it niffs like a ladies bog, because it *is* a ladies bog! He also says we are now in dead trouble if anybody catches us coming out of it, as you can get six months to life for being in the wrong toilet.

Naturally I want to know what we are going to do about this. Nocker thinks for a bit, then he gets a bright idea. He points to a couple of wigs what somebody plonks on a table and says,

"How about putting them things on and walking out of the lavvy looking like a pair of judies?" I tell him we will look very funny judies with our parkas and school keks on.

"Don't be a divvy, we have still got hold of the dresses what our old ladies give us, so we put them on, see!" he says back.

I want to know if you can get six months to life as well for wearing women's clothes, but he tells me to shurrup, and give him a hand with his zips.

Soon we are both all dressed up. We shove the parkas down our fronts to give ourselves a bulge and make it look realistic, and roll up our keks. I think our kicker shoes might give us away, but Nocker says not to worry, as nobody will notice nothing, seeing as how tarts' fashions get screwier all the time.

When we are ready, we go through the door walking like our bums are made of jelly, same as real judies do. Everything goes smashing at first, and we think we are getting away with it till who do we bump into but Duff Riley himself, in person, who has also come shopping with his mam, but manages to give her the slip.

Duff gives Nocker one look then he lets rip with a real dirty low-down wolf whistle.

"Hiya Gorgeous," he says, "how about coming out with us tonight?"

Nocker walks off with his nose in the air, letting on he hasn't heard a word of this and I follow him. But Duff won't take No for an answer. He comes on after Nocker, trying to chat him up, telling him he fancies him something rotten. Nocker starts walking quicker and quicker, till he sees the shop door. He makes a dive through this, with me right behind him.

But now it seems we are in more trouble, as it is not the way out like we think, but the way in, to one of C & A's windows. So there we are stuck, standing there with our backsides stuck out trying to look like real shop window dummies, with the whole of Church Street looking in at us.

Next thing, who should come along but Basher our beloved headmaster, and he has got Mrs. Basher with him too. She stops in front of us and begins eyeing Nocker up and down.

"My dear," she says to her old feller, "don't you think them shoes what are on the model look rather smart?"

Basher gives Nocker a good hard stare. Then he turns a bit pale.

"You know something?" he says to Mrs. Basher, "that dummy has got a face a bit like Yates who is a boy at my school, and a right pain in the seat of the keks, if you'll pardon the expression, loved one."

Mrs. Basher tells him not to think about school when it is holiday time, as it will only bring him out in them spots again. Then she says she has got to go in and get a pair of those shoes what Nocker is wearing, as she thinks they will do something for her, though what this would be we can't see, as she has got a face like the back of a corpy bus.

Then the both of them push off and we are left looking po-faced and wondering if we will have to stay in C & A's window the rest of our lives. But, all of a sudden, the door opens behind us and some shop judy leans in and grabs hold of Nocker by his foot.

We find out later what happens. It seems Mrs. Basher goes around creating to all the assistants as how she wants a pair of shoes like the ones she sees in the window, and of course they can't find none. So in the end they send someone to take Nocker's off of him, just to shut her up.

Nocker don't go too much for having his leg grabbed, as he is ticklish in them parts. He lets out one almighty screech, and then he takes off like the clappers with me close behind.

The shop judy yells the place down because she starts to think that C & A's is haunted, and that all the models are coming to life! But we keep on running till some feller with pin-stripes on his keks, what talks like he has a hot potato in his gob, gets hold of us by the lughole. Next thing the whole shop is alive with scuffers.

Of course it all sorts itself out in the end. They send out an SOS on the loudspeaker for our mams to come and collect us. These are proper narked for showing them up in front of all the other ladies from Scottie Road what are there, and they tell us,

"Just you wait till we get you home, son!"

The busies warn us as well telling us,

"We won't do yer this time lad, but watch it or youse is in dead lumber."

Mrs. Basher has got the biggest cob on of the lot, as she has set her heart on buying Nocker's shoes, and now she find she can't have them — no way!

And then what do you know? Next time we are in town and go past C & A's windows we see they have got a whole lot of kickers on show.

These are just like what Nocker is wearing, excepting they have a notice saying 'LATEST FASHION — ONLY £39.99'. The whole of Church Street is alive with judies, queueing all round the block for them.

Naturally me and Nocker go in to see the feller with the pin-stripe keks, right away, no messing. We ask him,

"How about giving *us* a slice of the action too Mister, as it is all our idea?"

'But he tells us to push off smartish, or he will call in the scuffers again, only this time they will nick us good and proper. So we have to split without getting nothing at all.

It makes you sick the way some of these big shops make their money, don't it?

3

Nocker Yates Goes to the Zoo

"Don't ever get yourself in the papers," says me Mam. The Yateses, whose blue-eyed baby boy Nocker is me best mate, think similar. They are very proud of the family name, what has always been good, except for the usual drunk and disorderlies every Saturday night, and a great uncle what gets hung at Walton one time. So when me and Nocker are front page news in the Liverpool Echo there is a big nark all round.

When this happens we are in the Mixed Infants, years ago. We are not mates yet, as we are both in different classes. Nocker is getting his education learnt to him by Miss Pringle, while a lady called Miss Scott is practising her karate chops on me behind the Wendy House. We never meet socially, except to sing nice hymns in the hall, or when we queue outside the bog at playtime for wee-wee's.

Then one day Nocker's teacher goes sick with food poisoning, as it seems she eats a school dinner by mistake. This means that her class has got to be split up all over the place, so Nocker and some of his mates come busting in to us, just when we are starting Music and Movement.

Music and Movements is where you all stand round an old clapped out loudspeaker. This makes a fizzing noise, and then tells you it is BBC Radio for Schools. After that some judy with a hot potato in her gob comes on and says you are to be a gnome, or maybe a fairy toadstool.

This time we are being trees for a change. I am standing there waving me branches about and hoping that no dogs come along, when all of a sudden, some kid behind me starts screeching blue murder. I turn round to see what's up, and there is Nocker with one of those 'I am innocent' looks on his face, what we all put on when we are in trouble.

The one what is doing all the screeching is somebody called Tina Maloney, who is the biggest snitch in the whole school. She is also pointing at Nocker, and keeps grabbing hold of her bum all the time. It seems that Nocker parks his chewy on the floor to keep it fresh while he is doing his poncing around and Miss Maloney plonks her rear end right in it. She has to be took away to the lady teachers' bog and got unstuck.

This means the end of the lesson and we never get to shed our leaves in Autumn, like the judy with the hot potato in her gob is asking us, which gets the teacher mad. She is madder still when Ma Maloney (Tina's old lady), comes up to school on the bounce next morning. She tells everybody that them was Tina's best Sunday go-to-meeting knickers what she had on, and she is going down to the office at 14 Sir Thomas Street about it.

So Nocker gets his spare parts chewed off, and told that he is a very bad boy indeed. They also tell him that he won't be allowed to bring any sweeties with him when we go to Chester Zoo next week, but only his packed lunch.

Nocker don't go for this at all, not one little bit, as he is a growing lad and needs to keep his strength up. But Miss won't change her mind. She even frisks him the day of the trip before we get on the bus and finds fifty pee what he stuffs in his shoe. So he gets on the coach with his sarnies only. I try to sit next to him, as I reckon that anyone what sticks Tina Maloney's bum up with chewy is worth getting to know, but they shove me some place else.

All the mums with curlers in their hair what are standing around watching, wave us good-bye and say, "Oo, don't they look lovely!" The bus rolls off and some old tart stands at the front of it and tells us to sing a happy song, and to please be sick in the bags provided — if we don't mind! This is a very muscle-bound old judy, besides being the headmistress, so we do our best to oblige. We start giving out with, "I'm going to the zoo, zoo, zoo and you can come too," so loud that by the time we get to Chester our tonsils are wore out.

Then they sling us off the coach and stand us in a long line so they can stick labels all over us with our names and other vital statistics on. Next we get given loads of papers with all crap about the animals and suchlike, which is screwy as they don't learn none of us to read yet. After that they tell us to shove off and look round and don't get lost, while the teachers go for a nice cup of tea.

We all make for the ice cream van first and then go and look at them monkeys with the pink behinds. All of us except Nocker that is. He has got no money, so he just wanders off on his own by himself, looking cheesed. We don't see him no more till hometime.

When I get on the bus again I go to the back seat, as everywhere else is full up. And who do I see sitting there but Nocker, and not only is he scoffing away at a great big bunch of bananas, but he has also got a huge gorilla sat next to him, who is wearing Nocker's school cap and has got one arm round his neck. Naturally I want to know what is going on and Nocker tells me the tale as follows.

It seems he is wandering round the zoo feeling like his stomach thinks his throat is cut, as he eats all his sarnies hours ago coming on the bus; when he sees this keeper what is carrying a bunch of bananas, going into a building. He hangs around for a while and when the keeper comes out again without the bananas and shoves off, Nocker pushes open the door of the building and goes in himself to have a look round.

Next thing he finds himself face to face with this monkey; Kong, as he starts calling him later. Nocker don't bat an eyelid as he has been used to the sight of his old feller for years, but it takes a while for Kong to get over the shock of clapping eyes on Nocker. In a while though, they get to being mates and Nocker swops him his school cap for the bananas what the keeper has brung.

After a bit he thinks it is time he went, so he says 'Tar-ra' to the monk and tries to shove off. Kong has got other ideas though about leaving Nocker, and when Nocker looks round there is the big gorilla following right after him. They go all the way to the bus and get on together. Nobody takes a blind bit of notice which is not as screwy as you might think, if you know what some of the kids in our school look like.

Then the bus takes us all the way back to the 'Pool and we get dumped outside the school gate. Me and Nocker wait till the last to get off, as we don't want nobody to know we have got Kong with us. But Tina Maloney is still hanging about. She is waiting to get Nocker, as she has still got a cob on about him messing up her best Sunday knickers. Soon as she sees him she goes up and kicks him real hard in the belly. She also tells him not to start anything back or she will snitch on him to Miss, and he won't half cop it in the neck.

Nocker don't say nothing back to her, as he is too busy holding on to his spare parts and bending double. But Kong gets real mad. He thinks Nocker is his best mate by now and nobody is going to do that to him and get away with it. He starts beating on his chest with both hands and next thing he has got hold of Tina Maloney and is shinning up the side of the school with her. When he gets to the roof he stuffs her half way down one of the chimbleys and pushes off smartish, leaving her with her nut sticking out at the top and yelling her head off.

Soon as Nocker see this, he forgets all about any damage what might have been done to his wedding gear.

"Come on Scouse," he shouts me, "time we wasn't here no more!"

We start to run and as we go along we can hear sirens and suchlike beginning to start up and there seem to be scuffers and fire engines dashing about all over the place.

Then we bump into Duff Riley who tells us that everybody thinks all the fuss is over somebody what just busts out of Walton Gaol, but he gives it as his own opinion, personal like, that it is aliens what land from outer space by UFO; and the authorities aren't codding on as they don't want no panic, but he isn't bothered himself as he is a proper hard knock.

While he is saying this, who should come round the corner sudden-like, but Kong, who is still wearing Nocker's cap. Duff takes one look and we get a front-row seat of what panic is all about as he goes white all over and takes off at sixty mph, shouting his head off for his Mam.

Kong seems real pleased to see us once again, but we are not quite so chuffed ourselves, as we reckon he is going to land us right in it sooner or later. We have a natter about what to do with him, and in the end Nocker says he will take him to his house and try and hide him there. Then in the morning he will get a paper round or something, till he makes enough money to pay Kong's fare back to Chester Zoo. He shoves off with Kong trailing behind him and I see the both of them up to Nocker's front door.

After they go in I hang about a bit, just to see if everything is OK. It is getting dark by now and I am thinking of pushing off myself, when I hear the noise of some woman screeching her head off inside the Yateses residence. Then this stops and everything is dead quiet, except for a kind of 'Klunk' sound.

Next thing Nocker's front door busts open again and his old lady comes busting through it out into the street. She is shouting all sorts of bad words, what a lady didn't oughta know really, and is also dragging Kong along by his hind legs. I happen to notice that Kong isn't wearing Nocker's cap no more.

It seems that Ma Yates is on her way to put fifty pee in the lecky meter as the lights conk and she bumps into Kong in the passage. She thinks it is Pa Yates coming back from the alehouse where he has been spending all the rent money, so she lands Kong one with her famous left hook, which is the pride and terror of Scottie Road.

The monk goes down for the count. Ma Yates drags him out into the street, as she is a most kind-hearted judy, and she wants to give

19

her ever-loving husband, as she thinks, some fresh air. She also wants to bring him round so as she can get cracking with round two.

But she is most put out when she finds out who she really has been battering. She starts screaming and fainting all over the place. The neighbours all come up to see what's up, and one of them calls the busies. These turn up in a black maria, put handcuffs on Kong and take him to the copshop, though what they charge him with nobody ever gets to find out.

Also, as bad luck would have it, there is some reporter feller snooping around the place, who starts sticking his long nose in asking people questions. In the end the whole story gets printed in the Liverpool Echo, late edition, front page.

Things become very rough for me and Nocker next morning when we show up at school. First we get battered something rotten, then the teachers tell the other kids that they are not to talk to us no more. But we don't mind this too much after a bit, as it is the start of our beautiful friendship and also leads to our great business partnership in the rag and bottle collecting as well as in the car minding business.

4

Nocker Goes in for Art

"Things is different in school nowadays, from when I was a girl," says me Mam. And she's not kidding, though if you says, "Youse is dead right there our Mam, they give up writing on slates when Queen Victoria kicked the bucket," she gets mad for some reason or other, and batters you.

Mind you she could be thinking of the letter we get given to bring home one time, from our beloved headmaster Basher:-

"Dear Parents,

Your baby boy has now got a chance of doing Art and Craft or Metalwork. Kindly put your thumbprint in the space provided for which what you want him to have, and get this brung back quick or else.

Yours truly, love and kisses etc.

"We will do Metalwork," Nocker tells me, "Art and Craft is strictly for puffs only. Also they might learn us how to make spare car keys, then we can move the motors of them fellers what don't pay up into our car-minding business, as we don't work for nothing."

But when he gets his letter home he runs into trouble as Ma Yates don't understand no more of what goes on in schools nowadays than what my old lady does. Nor does Old Man Yates neither, who gets in from work just as Nocker is explaining to his Mam what Art and Craft is all about.

It seems that he has been having business worries also, just now, and this stops him from listening proper to what Nocker is trying to say. Two ships have come up the river at once, which means the dockers have to set to and unload them immediate. They can't get to the alehouse till dinner-time at twelve o'clock and all hands suffer considerable, Nocker's old man as well. So, when he hears Nocker saying that Art and Craft is painting and suchlike, he gets hold of the wrong end of the stick.

He thinks Nocker is going to be learnt something useful at school for a change, like being able to put a few coats on the outside lavvy what needs it real bad. He says to shove his name down for that, then pushes off to get some ale down his neck quick, as they close at ten-thirty and it is nearly half-past five now, before Nocker can tell him any different.

Nocker is very cheesed about this. So am I, as I have to go in the same class as him, seeing he is me best mate, also he has the takings from this week's car-minding on him. I try to cheer him up though, by telling him we might get to painting some judies in the nude, just like proper artists do, but he says No Chance.

"Remember them sex lessons I signed up for last year?" he says back. "Well, the only cheap thrill I get *there* even, is when we cut up dead frogs and Duff Riley stuffs one inside the front of me keks."

When we get to the Art and Craft class, we find he is dead right. First thing we clap eyes on is a long skinny puff with a lot of nitty whiskers. This is Rembrandt the screwy art teacher, though why he is called Rembrandt nobody ever finds out, as it is not his proper name. This feller has got a whole lot of half-dead flowers stuck into jam jars and we have to paint pictures of these. Also, if there are any nude judies anywhere about the place, we don't get to see them.

Nocker gets fed up real quick. So when Rembrandt says, "Get on with your work quietly boys, while I go and see the headmaster," and pushes off for a quiet ciggy in the teachers' bog, he starts messing. First of all he has a few games of noughts and crosses with Duff Riley on the blackboard. Then he begins writing "EVERTON IS ACE" in blue paint, all over his drawing paper.

Rembrandt comes back while he is in the middle of this, and gets a proper cob on. He tells Nocker he will have to do another picture for him, at home, tonight. Naturally Nocker informs him that his union don't allow no unpaid overtime, but Rembrandt says to bring it in tomorrow first thing, or else he goes to Basher (our beloved headmaster). Basher is too tough for Nocker to handle, so he says back, "OK, Sir La, keep your 'air on, will do."

That night the both of us get cracking painting another drawing, in the shed where Nocker's old feller keeps his pigeons. We use a piece of hardboard, also some tins of Dulux what his big brother knocks off from work. It don't look too good by the time it's finished, but Nocker says it will have have to do. The pigeons don't help much either, as they keep dive-bombing the picture and we have to spread it around and hope people will think it is clouds in the sky and suchlike. We then wrap it up in a bit of brown paper tied with string.

Next morning, when we bring it back to school, we find it is early, so we take a walk round and about. Just as we go past the Walker Art Gallery, some feller in a hurry comes flying round the corner real quick. He don't look where he's going and bumps into Nocker so hard he sends him flying, making him drop the picture what he is carrying.

"Sorry son," says the feller.

"That's all right Mister, I don't break easy," Nocker says back. Then he sees that the feller has dropped a parcel what he was carrying, so he picks it up and hands it back to him, real polite. After that he picks up his own packet which is lying on the pavement, and we push off to school as it is now getting late.

When Nocker hands in his drawing and Rembrandt unwraps it our screwy art teacher nearly goes off his nut. He starts jumping up and down all over the place, screeching his head off like a big soft tart. He holds the picture for everybody to see and when Nocker takes a look at it he nearly swallows his chewy with shock.

Because the painting what Rembrandt is carrying on about is not Nocker's at all, but some screwy judy that's got both eyes on the same side of her head for a start. She is also in the nuddie, and is likewise going to have trouble at Marks and Sparks buying herself a bra what fits, as she has three you-know-what's!

Of course Nocker sees straightaway that his parcel must have got swopped by mistake with the feller's what knocks him flying outside the Art Gallery. He tries to tell all this to Rembrandt, who won't listen to one word he says and sends Nocker off to Basher for the stick. This is for drawing a dirty picture, also for insulting a great genius, as somebody has wrote the name P. Picasso across the painting and Rembrandt thinks it is Nocker, though who this same P. Picasso is nobody knows, as he don't play for Everton, nor even the Reds neither.

That evening when we are going home, we go past the Walker Art Gallery again, and we see a big queue what goes all round the building. Nocker's big brother is hanging about there too, waiting for a bet to come up. We ask him what all this is about and he tells us that they are waiting to see a picture what has just come over from Paris. This is by an artist what is very famous called P. Picasso, and is worth millions. Nocker's big kid knows about things like that, as he goes round them alehouses in Liverpool 8 where they have poets and suchlike, and is always bringing university judies back to the house, and sometimes fleas.

Soon as Nocker hears the name P. Picasso, he gives me the nudge to duck into the Art Gallery real quick. We manage to get past the queue before they can stop us and when we get inside we see a whole load of people staring at something. What is more, all these fellers and judies have got the sort of look on their faces what you usually see on the fans when Everton is beating Man. United six-nothing. The thing that they are all made up about is nothing less than Nocker's picture what he lost this morning, which is now hanging on the wall in a lovely gold frame.

"Right then," Nocker says to me as soon as we get outside again. "It seems that, as they have got my picture in there, we must have the real P. Picasso, none other, which is worth millions. So as they don't seem to know no different, this is where we clean up big."

We go back to his house, grab hold of the picture and then make for Castle Street, where they have them posh art shops. We go in one and a feller wearing pinstripe keks and a hot potato in his gob, comes up and asks what we want.

Nocker says to him, "We've got this real genuine P. Picasso painting what's worth millions really, but we can let youse have it for ten thousand quid as a favour."

The feller don't say nothing, but just looks hard at Nocker for a while. Nocker begins to lose his nerve and says "Alright Mister, we'll take fifty pee for it, if it's cash you're offering."

Then the Art shop feller says to wait there for a minute and goes into a little room at the back where we can hear him talking to somebody on the phone. The next thing there is a scuffer car pulling up outside and a whole load of flat hats start to pile out. Naturally we shove off quick, as our Mams tell us we must never talk to busies.

We go round the corner of Castle Street like the clappers and up Dale Street. The scuffers get back in their motor and drive after us. They chase us all the way to the Mersey Tunnel opening and along William Brown Street, where the museum is.

We make a dive to get into this, at least Nocker does and I get stuck in the swing doors and find myself nicked. I don't see Nocker no more till next morning, when we both meet waiting outside Basher's room, to get the stick for flogging fake P. Picasso's, and he tells me what happens to him.

It seems that while he is inside the museum he sees this big box in one of the rooms. He takes the lid off and gets inside to hide till the scuffers push off. Then somebody comes along and puts the lid back on again and starts carrying the box some place else while Nocker is still inside.

Nocker waits for a bit after they dump him down again. Then he reckons he will get out, as the heat should be off by now and he's busting to go to the lavvy. So he lifts the lid up and takes a peep. But there are a lot of fellers and judies all round the place, and these start screaming and fainting and suchlike.

It seems that the box, what Nocker parks himself inside, is one of them wooden overcoat things that they wear inside the Pyramids to keep the cold out; and everybody thinks he is King Tut's ghost come back to haunt them or something. Anyways they all push off immediate and Nocker climbs out of his box and makes for the bog. But he has a lot of trouble getting in it as there is a big queue in front of him because everybody what was in the same room with him wants to go to the lavvy at the same time, for some reason or other.

So, in the end we are landed with the real P. Picasso and can't think what to do with it. Rembrandt don't know this though. He goes off to the Art Gallery and stands looking at Nocker's picture for one whole hour with his gob open. After which he comes back and gives Nocker nought out of ten on his school report for Art.

But Old Man Yates is made up because Nocker does a real cracker of a job painting the outside lavvy. Also his Mam thinks Nocker has done the P. Picasso picture himself in class. She's dead proud about this and hangs it in the bog so that all her mates can look at it sitting down in comfort.

5

Nocker Yates and the Roman Soldier

"All roads lead to Rome," says me Mam, though what she's on about, nobody knows, and if you tell her she's talking wet, as Liverpool are playing in Paris this year, she gets mad and batters you. Even so, after what happens recent to me and me best mate Nocker Yates, she could be right at that.

It all starts one afternoon when the lads is having a quiet ciggy in the school bog. All of a sudden, Duff Riley comes rushing in saying we're to get back to class immediate, as there is an inspector on the premises.

"So," says Nocker, "them fellers don't scare me, no way," and he gets out another fag. But then Duff mentions that Basher, our beloved headmaster, has said he will chop anybody with his stick what don't move the seat of his keks smartish. So Nocker shoves the ciggy away quick, as he reckons smoking just might damage his health, like it says on the packet.

We see the inspector when we get back to class. He is a long skinny puff, standing next to the teacher and grinning like a divvy. Our teacher don't smile though, nor does Basher who is there as well. They look at us like we was a bad pong from the drain or something. Then they tell us to open our History books at page ninety-six and start copying.

This is all about the Romans as usual. Ever since we started school they seem to learn us nothing else except about these fellers what go about in night shirts all the time. In fact Nocker gets in serious trouble over this when we are Mixed Infants, as they give him some glue and stuff, and tell him to get cracking with a model of the Forum, which is a Roman picture house or something. He happens to park the glue on Miss Pringle's chair, and she sits in it. Her knicks get stuck to her you-know-what, and she has to go to the school clinic. They tell her that they can't unstick her till next morning, though why she gets mad and comes back and batters Nocker just because she has to put off a date with her boy friend that evening, we don't understand till years later.

Anyway, there we all are, going hard at it and working like the clappers copying out this stuff about the Romans. But the inspector don't seem pleased, not one little bit. He calls Basher over and tells him that we are being learned all the wrong way. Basher is narked when he hears this, and wants to know what other way is he expected to learn History to a bunch of dead-beats like us.

"Well," says the inspector, talking like he has got a hot potato in his gob, "if I was you, first of all I would dress these nice boys up as Roman soldiers to get them interested. Copying things from books all day can be very boring."

Duff Riley goes, "Hear, hear," to this, then wishes he hadn't when he sees the look on Basher's face. But the inspector presses on regardless.

"Next," he says, "I would take them on a trip to Deva. In fact that is a very good idea indeed, and I will organise it myself, personal, for next week." Then he pushes off, and after he gives Duff a good going over for yelling out in class, Basher follows him.

Soon as he goes we all start nattering about this Deva place, and wondering what it is. Duff claims it is a funny farm out Chester way, and his auntie gets sent there one time because she keeps saying she is a teapot. We take no notice however, as we reckon he is suffering from shock after the battering Basher gives him.

When next week comes though we find out that Deva is the Roman word for Chester. The inspector turns up with a clapped out old Mersey Passenger Transport bus and we all pile on board, with pack lunches made from leftovers in the school kitchen, what even the mice don't want to know about. The bus shoves off and the inspector starts giving us a talk about the Roman army, to get us interested. Soon everybody, Basher as well, has gone fast asleep.

We don't wake up till we get to Chester. Basher shouts us to pile off and line up in twos, so as he can march us round the place. But the inspector says, "No way!" to this. His idea is we go about on our own and make discoveries. Basher don't go for this, as he thinks it is all wet; also somebody might have told him about the time me and Nocker go to Chester Zoo and bring home this gorilla called Kong. But he can't do nothing except to tell us to shove off. Me and Nocker are made up, as we reckon now is our chance to find a good pitch for the car-minding and perhaps make ourselves a bob or two.

However we come real unstuck over this as, first of all, we lose our way and next thing we find ourselves on some kind of crummy old wall, with not a motor in sight. We are just wondering what to do when Nocker grabs hold of me arm and says, "Hey, what's that?"

I look to where he is pointing. There, standing all by himself is this feller what looks real weird. He is dressed up in some kind of armour stuff and has got on keks what look like me grand-da's comms. He also has a helmet on his head and is carrying a spear and a shield.

I tell Nocker that I think this must be one of the divvies who escapes from that funny farm they send Duff Riley's auntie to. But Nocker thinks different.

"I tell you what it is, Scouse," he says. "That is a mate of the inspector's what has got himself up like a Roman soldier to learn us history, like he was going on about in class. Come on, we'll have a bit of a laugh."

Next thing he goes straight up to the feller and shoves his arm up in the air, like he does at school when he is asking to be excused to the lavvy.

"Hail," he says, "All Hail, O mighty Caesar."

The feller turns round and before we know where we are he is giving Nocker a right proper gobful. Who the Hades does Nocker think he is, he asks, taking the mick and talking to a common ordinary squaddy like he was the Commander-in-Chief of the Imperial Roman Army, or something? He also says it is a good thing there isn't no officer, nor no centurion neither about the place, or we'd be given a good flogging, both of us. He keeps going on like this and his language is so bad it sounds worser than the old feller's, that time there is a brewery strike and all the alehouses have to shut down.

After a bit Nocker manages to get one or two words in edgeways and he apologises and says he is sorry. Then the feller calms down a bit and he tells Nocker, "That's all right son, but watch you lip or you're going to land yourself right in it." Next thing he starts looking us over, curious-like, and asking what we are doing there. He also wants to know why we are dressed like that, as he never sees nobody with clothes like ours before and are we natives? Nocker is narked at this and says back certainly not we are British. The feller says that was what he said first time, and are we stupid or something? Things start looking a bit awkward once more.

After a bit though we get to nattering more friendly and the queer feller starts telling us about himself. He says he is stationed at Chester with the Twentieth, whatever that means, and his name is Marcus Manlius Longinus, but we are to call him Shorty, same as his mates do. He also tells us that he is cheesed to his back teeth because Chester is a lousy dump, the weather is terrible, there is nothing to drink but British ale which is under the arm, and all the judies have got faces like the back end of one of Hannibal's elephants. In fact, he would give anything to be back in Civvy Street, at his old job which is the chariot minding outside the Colosseum in Rome, where you can make a bomb when the big games are on, like Lions v. Christians. Even so, he says, it is better here than on the Wall.

We ask him about this Wall place, and he tells us it is the worstest posting in the whole Empire. It seems some Emperor builds it one time, to stop all the Haggises busting in and causing trouble at Wembley and suchlike places. Ever since, the army sends all its bad lads there, what won't behave, to learn them some manners. Shorty says it is a terrible hole with no ale and no judies and the rain keeps on hissing down all the time, though he don't say hissing.

Also you can't get no sleep at nights, as you are on stag all the time, keeping your eyes skinned for trouble and hoping no Haggis arrow don't land in your guts sudden-like. Shorty claims he's been sent there two times already for flogging his kit and so forth; also he thinks he will have to go again, as they are bound to find out he knocks off a barrel of Falernian wine from outside the officers' mess, so as all his mates can have a bevvy. This time, too, he thinks he has had it, as he knows there is a Haggis arrow with his name and number on it waiting for him up there; and then his ghost will be walking up and down for always, doing everlasting guard duty, just to punish him for having been a bad lad all his life.

All the while that he is talking Nocker keeps on giving me the nudge and the wink, as if to say, "There, what did I tell you, it's a mate of the inspector's giving us the Roman history lark." But me, I am not so sure.

First, Shorty don't look the sort of feller what has been to college and university. Although he's just over five foot tall he is burned black all over with the sun and seems a proper hard knock. Next, all the time he is talking about getting the chop he has a look in his eye, the sort of look I have seen on someone else, but I can't think who, or where. Be that as it may, while I am listening to him I keep getting this cold, shivery feeling, though the sun is shining fit to crack the flags.

Then, all of a sudden, Shorty stops his nattering and says he's got to go. He shakes us both by the hand and tells us it's been a real pleasure meeting us. After that he does the about turn and marches off, and as he goes he starts singing, like this:—

> 'I don't want to join the Legion,
> I don't want to go to Gaul;
> I think I'd rather stay
> Around the Appian Way,

Living on the earnings of a Sabine lady.
I don't want to go to Britain,
No, by Pollux, I'd turn blue;
I'd sooner stay in Pompei,
In dear old, dear old Pompei . . .'

When he gets to here he stops and gives us a wave. "So long me old mates," he shouts, "Be seeing youse."

Next thing, something happens which is real weird and frightens the keks off of me. First, I get this sort of buzzing in me ears and then me heart is thumping away like a steam engine. Also I find I am yelling out words that I never hear before, and don't understand what they mean now.

"Salve," I am shouting, "O Marcus Manlius Longinus, Salve!" while Nocker is bawling something out as well, what sounds like, "Ave atque Vale, Ave atque Vale!"

Shorty gives us one more wave of his hand and then he goes round the corner so quick it looks like he vanishes into thin air; just as the inspector comes along.

The inspector takes one look at me and Nocker screeching the place down and his gob drops open wide. Then, before we know where are are, he grabs us both by the arm and gives us the bum's rush back to the bus, where Basher is hanging about having a quiet ciggy.

"There you are headmaster," the inspector says to him, sounding real made up, "what did I tell you? Only one hour in Chester and here are these boys already talking in Latin!" The he starts going on to Basher about how he hears me say, "Goodbye, God bless," in Roman and Nocker has been shouting, "So long, I'll be seeing you," in the same lingo.

Naturally Basher don't believe a blind word of it. He tells the inspector that we have been talking in Scouse more like, Vauxhall Road perhaps, or it could be a touch of the East Garston; and the inspector, who is a foreigner from the Wirral, wouldn't understand them sort of things. Anyway they keep on arguing about it all the way back to the Pool and nobody can get a wink of sleep this trip with the racket they make.

Nocker tells me that the inspector is a real divvy and his mate what we meet on the wall is a nut case too. I don't say a word back to this, but I am busy thinking hard.

First I remember where I see that look in Shorty's eyes before. It is when my cousin, who is in the Royal Greenjackets, is going back from his leave to Ulster, and tells us he *knows* he is due to be killed this tour of duty. Next, if it really was a pal of the inspector's all dressed up to learn us History, why don't the inspector let on about it?

So, one way or the other, I don't think I want to tell Nocker that, in my opinion, we have just been talking to the ghost of a Roman soldier what has been dead nigh on two thousand years!

6

Nocker Yates Goes to Paris

"Never go abroad," says me mam, "there's nothing there but a load of foreigners what can't talk English proper and land you right in it."

She gives all this crap to me and Nocker Yates who is me best mate, when we ask if we can go to Paris with the school; though she don't know nothing about it really, as the furthest she ever goes is across the water to New Brighton, to play Bingo. But, come to think of it, the way things happen she turns out to be right at that.

It all starts when we get given a letter to bring home from our beloved headmaster Basher.

"*Dear Parents (this says),*

There is going to be an educational journey in the summer holidays. If you wish your baby boy to go on same, kindly shove your thumb-print in the space provided and have this brung back quick.

With love and kisses,
your truly etc."

All the lads say, "No chance," at first. This is because they remember last year's trip, when we have to live in tents, with the wind blowing round the seat of our keks all the time. Also Basher brings along his ever-loving Mrs. Basher and she is ten times worser than what he is.

Then Duff Riley gets to hearing something. He comes into the bog one playtime when we are having a quiet ciggy and gives us the tale.

"It seems we are going to start doing French next term," Duff says, "as they pack in trying to learn us English as a bad job. So this school trip what they are on about is to Paris, to get us in the mood, like."

The lads all say three cheers to this, naturally, as we fancy a bit of the froggy Oo-la-la stuff for a change, what we already read about in the dirty bookshop behind Cazneau Street. Nocker is special keen to have a bash, as he thinks we might be able to muscle in on the foreign car minding racket also.

But when I get home and ask, "Can I go?" the answer is, "Nothing doing." My old lady, for a start, won't hear of it. She says I am a growing lad now and she wouldn't trust me in one of them rude foreign places, not even if I was sewn up for the winter four months ahead of schedule.

Nocker too has a spot of trouble about getting permission. It seems that his old feller has been doing a spot of clubbing, after the alehouses shut down for the night. He goes to this place called the Follies de Paris, or something, which is full of judies dancing round in nothing but two balloons and a load of goose pimples. He is so disgusted that he won't allow his baby boy anywhere near a place what has suchlike goings on all the time. And he don't change his mind, not even after he takes Nocker's catty along with him next night to burst the balloons and teach them a lesson for being dirty, and finds out, when they give him a gobfull, that they aren't French at all, but come from Toxteth.

Then Ma Yates gets in on the act. She gets a cob on because the scuffers knock her old man off for doing this, and she gets shown up in front of the neighbours when he is brung home in the Black Maria, and it's not Saturday night.

So she says Nocker *can* go to Paris after all, just to spite him. This makes my old lady change her mind as well, so it now seems as if we are heading for a spot of the wine, women and song malarkey, and things are looking good for us. They start to look even better when we find out that Mrs. Basher can't make it this time, and is leaving her ever-loving husband to go it on his own.

But you might know that anything what our school does is a dead loss and also under the arm. First we all get very sick on the boat, as Duff Riley buys some French ciggies and hands them round and we find out they don't even come from a healthy camel.

Things are last when we get there, too. Basher brings along Rembrandt, the screwy art teacher with the nitty whiskers, to help him; and he is such a divvy that he gets us lost, each time we go out. This don't matter really though, as they never take us anywhere near the X certificate stuff; all we get shown is art galleries and museums and suchlike. The only time we get anything like a cheap thrill is when we see a statue of some judy what is topless, and even that has got both of its arms broke off.

Then Mrs. Basher gets to remembering, back in the Pool, that her Basher has been here before. This is during the war when he liberates the place from the Germans, who push off like the clappers the minute they know he is coming, as they would sooner have the

Gestapo any day of the week. Mrs. Basher also knows he can find his way round, as he speaks the Froggy lingo real good, so she zooms over immediate just to keep her eye on him.

The minute she gets here she don't let him out of her sight, not one minute, nor us neither. We know now that there won't be no wine, nor no women neither, and even when Nocker starts to sing one time she tells him to shut his gob, or else.

So all the lads are dead chuffed when it gets to the last day and it is time to go home. They get a bit narked though when they find their train don't leave till the afternoon and they have got one more museum trip laid on for them in the morning.

Rembrandt is telling them all about it when me and Nocker roll in for our breakfast, half an hour late as we sleep in a bit. He starts jumping about and screeching the place down like a big soft tart when he sees us, for keeping him waiting. Then he says he can't hang around no more, but he will be in the Louvre round the corner from the hotel and we are to pick him up there when we have finished eating.

After he shoves off I tell Nocker I don't know what he is on about; but he tells me back that Louvre is the French for lavvy.

"You know what a divvy he is," Nocker says. "Well, most like he forgets to go when he gets out of bed, so now he has to make up for lost time. There is a public bog at the end of the street, so we will meet him there like he says."

But when we find the place though and go down the steps we don't find him, no way. There is nobody around except a little old French judy, which don't seem right in a gent's toilet, who is sitting at a table what has got a saucer full of money on it and is knitting her head off.

Anyhow we hang about for a bit, but nobody shows up. Then Nocker gets cheesed with waiting and says, "Let's go." We make to go up the steps again, but as we pass the little old judy she starts waving her arms at us and pointing to her saucer. We don't know what this is all about, but Nocker says perhaps she wants us to take some money, as a good-bye present. We each get hold of a handful and this gets her waving her arms even more and jabbering away like the clappers. So as we think this means perhaps we haven't took enough, we both make another grab at the saucer and this time we scoop in the lot!

Next thing she is starting to scream the place down. One of them French scuffers what go around the place wearing guns and gaiters hears the racket and comes down to see what it's all about. Soon as we see *him*, me and Nocker duck out of the place, real quick.

I just run along the street, but Nocker has got to box clever. He sees that the French busy has parked his bike against some railings, so he hops on it and rides off.

But before he gets very far he sees Basher coming along the pavement towards him, with Mrs. Basher. And, also, there is another judy with him too, what looks about the same age as Mrs. Basher, but don't look much like her otherwise; as this tart, who is French, is a real smart looker, while Mrs. Basher has got a face like the back end of a corpy bus.

It seems that this judy, what is called Fifi, knows Basher from years back; so when she sees him from the other side of the road she calls out to him, "Allo, my cherry," or something like that and comes over to have a word with him. She tells Mrs. Basher that she meets her beloved husband during the war and Basher is so busy trying not to let it slip out that he and Fifi get together first at one of them places where tired soldiers go for a nice lay-down that he don't notice Nocker careering about the place on a French scuffer's bike.

But Nocker sees him and does a quick about turn to go the other way. When he gets back to the bog though he finds the scuffer waiting for him. He tries to do a crafty swerve past him, and next thing he is shooting down the bog steps. The brakes on the bike are wonky, so he can't stop himself and has to go riding round and round at the bottom till the bike does a skid, sudden-like, he goes over the handlebars and ends up head first in one of the lavvo pans.

This is not nice, as they are not using any of that stuff what goes round the hidden bend over in Paris, yet. Also, after Nocker gets himself unstuck he finds the French busy all ready to go for him for nicking his bike and robbing the old woman. But when he gets a bit closer to Nocker he changes his mind for some reason, as perhaps he finds the ponk a bit fierce for his liking and pushes off immediate.

Basher too is having his problems, trying to explain to Mrs. B. how he comes to learn French so good off of Fifi. He is so busy at this that he don't have no spare time to give Nocker the stick for riding a bike on the pavement and suchlike.

Even so Nocker is very cheesed, as the French lavvo pong takes a long time wearing off and each time he takes a walk down Scottie Road after he gets home somebody goes to the Corpy and moans about the drains. But, as me Mam says, you ask for trouble when you go near them foreigners, what are dead ignorant. No wonder they call it the Common Market, says me Mam.

7

Nocker Yates and the Fourth Dimension

"The female of the species is more deadlier than the male," says me Mam. Which means, after you change it to proper English from hot potato in the gob talk that fellers can be a pain in the seat of the keks sometime, but tarts are far worse. Like the judy we get to be our teacher one time, for instance.

We all know we have trouble the minute she sticks her nut round the classroom door. For a start she is seven foot tall at least and has got a face like the back end of a corpy bus, with great big muscles bulging through the sleeves of her frock. She comes clumping in on her big flat feet and stands looking at us like we was bad pongs from a drain or something. Then she tells us to get cracking with our English, as she has got to fiddle about with the register.

Naturally we start messing after a bit, same as we do with all the new teachers. I have a go first. I lift me desk lid up and let it drop again with a great big bang. Then I say, "Sorry Miss, couldn't help it, it was an accident, honest," and smile at her, real pleasant.

Next thing, before I know what is happening, she is down on me and has got a hold of me earhole, which she starts trying to twist off. This is not nice and I tell her so. I also say to her that I am bringing me mam up to the school about it. She says straight back that she will bring her mam up too and her mam who is ninety-seven and blind and crippled will sort *my* old lady out, any day of the week. Then she goes back to her table and I rub me ear, which is swole up considerable.

Duff Riley has a bash next. He feels like a quiet ciggy so he goes out and asks to be excused to the lavvy. When she says, "No, go and sit down!" he starts clutching hold of himself and saying he can't wait, as he is nearly doing it in his keks. But she just grabs his arm and shoves him back in his seat so hard his behind nearly busts off. Then she says she is real sorry that a big boy like him isn't potty trained yet, but will he just kindly boil it until playtime. Naturally we are most shocked to hear a lady talking so common.

After that we keep quiet for a bit, till Nocker thinks he will try a spot of germ warfare. First he lets a proper ripe one go, real sly, then he starts looking round him, all innocent like and sniffing, as if to say, "Who done that?"

The lads play up immediate. They start jumping up and down and yelling, "Ah eh Miss, there aren't half a ponk in here, can we have the windows open, somebody's done it in his keks!" and suchlike.

Next thing she shouts, "Silence!" so loud all of our lugholes get blown in. Then, soon as a ton and a half of plaster stops falling from the ceiling, she tells us she will keep the whole class in if the boy what done that disgusting thing don't own up straight away.

Nockers knows he can't land the lads in it, so he stands up and tells her it was him. This always works with divvies like Rembrandt, the screwy art teacher, who just pats you on the back, tells you you are a good boy for being honest and lets you off. But not this judy.

She says he will have to stay behind after four o'clock, for one whole hour. And when Nocker says that his union don't allow no unpaid overtime, she says back he had better belt up quick or she will batter him so hard his grandchildren will feel it. After that we stay quiet till hometime.

Next morning Nocker's old lady comes up on the bounce. She is narked about Nocker being kept in, as she reckons he is delicate and too much school might harm his health. Also she wants him back home punctual yesterday, to shift in ten cwts of smokeless what the coalman dumps in the back entry.

She comes busting in to work Miss Coplady over, before going down to the office to have a moan about the cruel way her baby boy is being treated. But when she claps eyes on our teacher she stops dead in her tracks and goes white all over. And when Miss Coplady asks her what she wants she just says, "Er, I only come up to see how he's getting on with his work, like." Then she pushes off like the clappers.

Naturally we are most surprised at this, till we find out that Nocker's old lady and Miss Coplady have met before. This is before our teacher goes to college, when she is WPC Coplady, a scuffer judy. She runs in Nocker's mam one time, with one hand only, for being bevvied and, also, for chucking bricks through the windows of the Trustee Savings Bank because they won't give her a personal loan for money to spend in the alehouse. So now we know we really have had it, as anybody what can run Ma Yates in with two hands, even, is not to be messed with. All we can do is to pray for the school holidays or death, whichever comes first.

And she starts getting worse all the time too. First, we have to to work so hard our fingers get wore out right down to the bone. Next, she keeps coming into the school bog at playtime and interfering with us when we are having our quiet ciggy. And then one day she tells us, right out of the blue, that she is going to stop writing the date on the blackboard for us to copy in our books each morning as this is making us too lazy. We have to do it by ourselves and get it right. Anyone what don't stays behind and copies it out one hundred times.

This comes real hard on one of the lads who is called Jimmy Maloney. He is a bit slow; in fact one time they are talking about sending him to the silly school. But, when we begin having lessons on the telly he starts to pick up considerable. It seems he can remember everything what he sees on the box for some reason or other, nobody knows why, seeing as he is a bit of a divvy, otherwise. But this don't help him to get the date right, no way, and Miss Coplady is always on about it to him, picking on him every minute of the day and keeping him in, time after time.

Then, one morning, when she comes up behind him to give him a poke in the back and nag him, like usual, she changes her tune, sudden-like.

"Why James," she says, with her voice sounding like a rusty gate what somebody oils, with the way she tries to keep it soft and sweet, "Why James, you've got it right at last. What a good boy you are."

Jim's face goes very red as he don't go much for being called James, which he reckons to be fruity. Also he knows that she isn't pleased really as she would much sooner keep on chewing his spare parts off. But he keeps on getting the date right all week, till Friday comes. Then he lands right in it, once again.

"You silly, stupid boy," Miss Coplady yells at him, after she takes a look at his book Friday morning. "You've put down next Sunday's date. Even an idiot like you knows we don't come to school of a Sunday." And she goes at him worse than ever, also she makes him stay in and write out the date *two* hundred times, as she thinks he is taking the mick out of her.

Me and Nocker feel sorry for Jim so we wait behind outside school till he's finished, then we walk him back to his house.

"Youse is a right divvy," Nocker tells him as we go along. "What makes you do a screwy thing like that? You know she's out to get you!"

Then Jim says something back to this, what we think is proper weird. "That feller on the telly must have got it wrong," he tells me and Nocker. Naturally we ask him what he's on about and he gives us this tale.

"You know the way how I can remember everything what I see on telly. Well, I am watching ITV news the other night and then this feller comes on with the weather. I notice that when he says it's going to hiss down tomorrow he gives the date as well, so when it comes next morning I find I can write it down in me book without making no mistake. But yesterday evening he gets it wrong and lands me right in it with *her*."

"Them fellers on the telly don't make no mistakes," says Nocker back to him. "They give them their cards otherwise. You must have fell asleep and dreamt it all."

"No way," Jim tells him. "Just before the weatherman shows up they are showing the big game. I am not asleep when I see the opposition striker shove it past our goalie and put Liverpool out of the Cup; in fact I am wide awake and crying me eyes out. That was no dream; worse luck!" Then as he gets to where he is going he says, "Tar-rar," and goes in his house.

All the way home I keep getting this funny feeling that Jim says something what is real screwy and don't add up proper, but I can't think what it is. I tell Nocker about it, but he says to take no notice as Jim is a good skin but a bit off his cake sometimes.

Even so I don't seem to be able to get this feeling out of me nut and I have still got it when I am watching ITV news Saturday evening and they are showing bits from the quarter final. And, soon as I see the opposition striker beat Liverpool's goalie to score the winner, I know what it's all about. I jump to me feet and rush out of the house, looking for Nocker. We bash into each other in the middle of the road where he is belting along like the clappers to find me.

"You see the big match just now?" he asks. "Too right," I say back, "just like Jimmy Maloney. Only *he* sees it Thursday, two days before it happens." Nocker shouts me to move the seat of me fat keks and we take off for Maloney's place like two fellers what are full of Heinz beans and are looking for a lavvy real desperate.

Jim is in his front room when we get there, sitting with his Nan who looks after him ever since his Mam and Dad kick the bucket when he is a baby. She has got to be as screwy as him, as both of them are looking at the telly and neither of them don't seem to know the programme they are watching, which is Coronation Street, isn't on till next Monday.

We get Jim outside and ask him what it's all about. It takes a bit of time for him to catch on, as he don't seem to know what we are on about for a while. Then, after the penny drops, he tells us what happens.

It seems that he is looking in last Thursdsay night waiting for the weather man to come up with tomorrow's date when the set, which is an old clapped out black and white job, packs it in, like it is always doing. So he gives it the usual treatment, a whacking great thump and, sudden-like, it gives out an enormous big bang what frightens the keks off of him. Next thing it comes on again but this time it is so bright and clear it is like new. Then it shows him the footie match what me and Nocker watch just now.

"You know something?" Nocker says to him, "youse is dead jammy."

"Why?" asks Jim.

"Because you have now got the only fourth dimension telly in the whole world. That thump what you give it makes it show things that happen in the future, just like science fiction and Dr. Who and suchlike. This is where we clean up real big."

Me and Jim ask him what he's on about.

"Football pools, you pair of dickheads!" Nocker says. "We get the weekend results Thursday night from Jim's telly, shove in the coupon Friday and come Saturday we are all millionaires. We can retire before we leave school."

Jim thinks this is a real cracker idea. So do I, at first, but then I get to thinking about it and I am not so sure.

"Hang about," I say to Nocker, "youse is forgetting something. Don't you have to be eighteen before they let you do the pools?"

"So," says Nocker. "What's to stop us getting some feller who *is* eighteen to fill the coupon in. We tell him what to put, give him a bob or two for his trouble and collect the rest. No problem."

"That's what you think." I say back. "And what if the feller we ask goes and rings up the funny farm after we tell him we have got a 4D telly what shows the future and they come for us in a plain van? Nobody, but nobody, is going to believe us."

Just then we hear this voice from behind us. "I might believe you," it says. "Why not give it a try?"

We turn round and we see a feller standing there what seems to have been listening to us talking for quite a bit. This feller is called Mr. Forehigh and he has got a shop behind Great Homer Street Market what sells tvs and videos and such-like. We don't know much else about him except that the busies do him once for having stolen stuff in the back of his place, but he manages to wriggle out of it.

"So me lucky lads," he says to us, "you reckon you have got a telly what can see into the future, do you? Well, I'll tell you what. We'll give it a little try-out, shall we? You just give me all the weekend scores this Thursday and if I check them out to be one hundred percent on the ball me and you lot are in business. Then I fill in the week after next's coupon for you and give me name on it and after we split sixty forty. The sixty is for me, of course, as I am doing all the work. Okay?"

Nocker tells him that it is not okay at all and he is robbing us rotten, seeing as how it is our set in the first place. But Forehigh just says to take it or leave it as that is his final offer. So in the end we have got to take it, though none of us like the look of him, not one little bit.

Anyhow we give him the scores on Thursday like he asks for and when Saturday comes they are all dead right of course. But after that it seems like he disappears into thin air, as he don't come round to arrange for the next load of footie results. We go round to his shop to find out what he's playing at but we don't see hide nor hair of him there neither, what's more the place is all shut down.

Then we clock him on Thursday afternoon. He is coming out of Jim's place, carrying their black and white telly. We ask him what his game is and he gives us a smile what would put a crocodile off his dinner.

"Just doing me day's good deed, like when I was a boy scout once," he says. "I think it is a real cruel shame that a sweet little white-haired old lady should have to soldier on with a clapped out job like this so I give her, out of the goodness of me heart, a brand-new 24 inch colour set in exchange for it, with nothing to pay, and she is proper made up."

We tell him that he don't fool nobody with that do-good line of talk and he is a lousy cheat what wants to rob us of our winnings. We also say that we will split on him to the busies.

"Oh yeah!" he says back. "And can't I just see the scuffers believing every word when you tell them that somebody nicks your 4D telly what shows next week's football results. How about the funny farm then?"

Nocker says some bad words to him, about how his father never gets married to his mother and suchlike, but Forehigh only laughs. Then he shoves the set in the back of his van and drives off and we don't expect to see him, never no more.

However he is back the very next day, as it happens, in a right paddy. He goes to Jim Maloney's place and says we are all having him on about the old black and white telly showing the future. It seems that, after he plugs it in, it don't show nothing at first so he gives it a big bang to make it work. But all he sees then, when it comes on, is some kind of history play, which he thinks is dead boring and under the arm, about a load of fellers with long hair wearing funny clothes trying to do other fellers with short hair. So he dumps the old telly in Jim's Nan's front room and goes off in a proper nark with the colour set.

Of course we realise what happens. The bang Forehigh gives the telly changes it round from giving you the future, and it now shows what went on in historical times. Jim and his Nan keep on watching it, though she don't notice nothing different as she thinks every programme what they see is Granada and when some king comes on what is being tried for having his head chopped off she tells Jim that it must be 'This Is Your Life' with Eamon Andrews.

Next thing what happens is that Miss Coplady, who can't forget about Jim putting down Sunday's date to take the mick out of her, as she thinks, puts his name down to go to the silly school and tells Basher, our beloved headmaster, that this is the right place for him as he is the worst divvy in the whole school.

The office has got to send an inspector along to see what Jim is like and this feller takes Maloney on one side for a long chat. Jim starts telling him all about the barneys with the old-fashioned long-hairs and greases, what he watches on the telly. The inspector says that these are called Cavaliers and Roundheads and they are fighting in something what he calls the Civil War, though it don't look too civil, the way they keep shoving long poles with spikes on the end into each other.

Anyway, he goes to Miss Coplady and says that Jim is a very bright boy, as he seems to know more about history than any other lads he meets in a long, long time. He also gives her a right rollicking for wasting his time and then he goes to Basher next and says what is he doing having dozy teachers like that in his school and he ought to ashamed of himself.

So Basher, first chance he gets, makes sure that Miss Coplady is shifted to another school and we get Rembrandt, the screwy art teacher, to learn us instead; who is a right soft touch.

Me and Nocker go along to Jim's place quite often to have a look at his 4D telly. Just now it is showing all about this king called Charlie Two and also a judy named Nellie something or other. Most of the action seems to take place at night and as they only have candles in them days and no lecky light, we don't see everything what happens. But we see enough to find out that when me Mam says that history is all bunk she is not kidding, no way!

8

Nocker Yates and the Garden Festival

"You are nearer God's heart in a garden" says me Mam, "more than anywhere else on earth." Which is screwy, seeing as we haven't got no garden, only a window box which has got so many weeds it wouldn't touch nobody's heart.

Mind you, it does touch the rentman's head when he comes calling for the back thirteen weeks what is owing. This is because the old feller feels like some fresh air after coming back bevvied from the alehouse. So he shoves his nut out of the winder and knocks the box right on the rentman's bonce. Not only is this one's language most choice when he comes round but he also raises our rent by four quid.

Me and Nocker Yates don't go much on this spade and horse manure malarkey neither, as they give it us as a school lesson one time. The lads moan considerable when they find they have to work like the clappers digging up the playground so as Basher, our beloved headmaster, can grow cabbages and suchlike for Mrs. Basher.

So when this International Garden Festival lark comes up none of us wants to know, as it costs the earth for a ticket and also they have got these security fellers with radios all over the place what stop you climbing in. Me, Nocker, Duff Riley and the others say, "No way are we spending a fortune just to niff at some lousy flowers what you can nick from the cemetery for nothing."

Then our beloved headmaster Basher gets in on the act. He tells us in the school hall that we are going to this same garden festival as an educational visit. The lads think that anything is better than doing English and suchlike, till he says that the trip is scheduled for Saturday and anybody what don't turn up will have him to deal with, come Monday. It's no use telling him neither that the union don't allow no unpaid overtime, as he is so tough that even the Gestapo pack in and go home when he invades them on D-Day, in the war.

Our old fellers likewise moan considerable when we tell them they have to cough up one pound fifty for us to get in. But they know they can't mess Basher around, as they was learned by him too, one time. So it just means the alehouses will be down on their takings this weekend. Our mams have got a cob on also, as they have to make us pack lunches because the school kitchen closes down Friday afternoon.

We find Basher waiting for us outside the school Saturday morning. There is the usual clapped out corpy bus they always send on these jobs, what fails its MOT years ago, also we see Rembrandt the screwy art teacher, who is helping out, though what use he is nobody knows as he is the biggest divvy outside of the funny farm.

Just as we are piling on the bus the school secretary, who is doing overtime too but getting paid for it, comes out and tells Basher some big cheese inspector down at the office wants him on the blower, urgent. So Basher has to tell Rembrandt to take over and he will join us later, also to see everybody behaves, especially that boy Yates.

We are made up about this, as you can mess with Rembrandt. The minutes the bus starts some of the lads go to the back seats and light up a quiet ciggy. The rest of us begin dinging on the bus bell, or opening the windows and yelling things out of them, like, "Eh Missus, yer backside just fell off," to a lady jogger, and so on.

Then Nocker starts cobbing tomatoes from his pack lunch at people on the pavement. Next I manage to cop an old woman on the seat of her fat keks with a rock cake, which must be most painful knowing my old lady's baking. And Jimmy Maloney scores bullseye on the spike of some tart's umbrella with a doughnut, after she puts it up to keep off a rain shower.

But we pack it in when Duff Riley hits a scuffer on his helmet so hard with an orange that he falls off of his bike. The busy is hopping mad and takes down the bus number in his notebook, so we know we are for it sooner or later.

We get to the Garden Festival at last and Rembrandt says, "Now boys, everybody off the coach quietly, follow me and don't get lost." His idea, after we get through the turnstile, is that we all go round together while he tells us about the pretty flowers, so as we can draw them in school, Monday. But the lads think this is wet, so first chance we get we stand still and let him go round a corner on his own still chunnering to himself about beautiful nature, with everybody looking at him and wondering where he escapes from.

After this Duff Riley finds he is starving, as he cobs his sarnies, like everybody else, out of the bus window. So he goes up to this Danish ice cream stall and asks for a cornet. The man holds one out to him and says, "Eighty pee, please." Duff says back that this is daylight robbery and he can stuff his cornet where the monkey puts its nuts, as he thinks the feller sounds foreign and won't understand. But the ice cream man understands English real good and he jumps across the counter and gives Duff a fourpenny one across the lughole.

Some security men see this happen and, next thing, they take to following us round so close they are breathing down our necks, as they think we are out to give trouble. We find this most embarrassing and give them the slip soon as we can by ducking into a tent.

This turns out to be a place what is all about looking after your health. There are fellers and judies in tracksuits who give you loads of bumpf about not smoking and eating all-bran to make you go to the lavvy real good. Also they have got machines to do exercises on and over one side is a table with computers on it.

These ask you personal questions like how old your family is when they kick the bucket and how many fags you smoke and suchlike. Then it works out how long it will be before you go for a crap yourself, though speaking personal I would sooner let this come as a nice surprise.

Duff has got to start his messing again, of course. He tells his computer that his mam is eleven and his dad four when they shove off, also that they plant his grand-da in Anfield Cemetery when he is one hundred and ninety-three.

Then the thing starts talking dirty. It wants to know how often Duff has sex and he says back, "Thirty-four times a day," which is not true really, but the computer don't know this and next thing it goes Wham-Bang, blows its fuse and all blue smoke comes pouring out of it.

The tracksuit fellers and judies think me and Nocker do this, as Duff does a crafty slide out of sight. They begin chasing after us to batter us and we have to go like the clappers to get away, as they are real fit with all the running to the lavvy they do after eating the all-bran stuff. By the time we shake them we are nackered good and proper.

So we go into another tent what has got seats in, for a rest. We plank our fat bums next to a very little judy what is reading a book and sucking a lollipop with one hand and playing with her ball with the other. There is also some kind of school concert going on, so we watch another little judy in the orchestra who is playing her violin and blowing chewy bubbles and we make bets whether this will bust and go 'Splat' all over her gob.

But after a bit we can't stand no more, as they keep playing this Radio 3 stuff what sounds like tomcats with bellyache. Also the little judy has stopped blowing bubbles and just sits there looking cheesed. So we reckon the heat will be off now and get up and push past all the people who go, "Sh, sh!" at us, as they are listening to the music which they seem to think is real cracker.

When we get outside though, there is more trouble, for not only is Basher, who has got shot of the big cheese inspector there, but also Rembrandt, the ice cream man, the scuffer that Duff cobs on the nut and the keep fit fellers and judies and so on. These are all going on to Basher about something or other, no prizes for guessing what, and we think it is time we made for the wide open spaces, immediate.

We are standing around, outside the Garden Festival somewhere a bit later and wondering what to do, when we hear music. We go round a corner and there we see the sad-looking little bubble-gum judy from the concert again. She is outside this railway station place playing her violin and all the people coming off the trains to go to the festival keep putting money in her tin and going "Ah" as she is a pretty little judy and plays good too, not the classical crap this time, but proper music like 'The Yellow Submarine' and suchlike. And with her as well is the very same little judy we sit next to, still playing with her ball, which when I look at close is a very screwy ball what is more pineapple shaped than round and dirty black, likewise.

Then the people stop coming off the train so the older one packs in playing and starts counting the money. She has got twice as much as me and Nocker make car-minding on a good day, but she still looks cheesed. So me and Nocker are dead curious and we go over and ask what the score is.

They tell us they are two sisters and their names are Satu and Sanna. We want to know why they have got screwy names like that and they say back it is because their mother comes from Finland.

I say, "How come you speak English so good when youse is foreign?" and she says back that she *is* English really, as her father comes from a place called Letchworth Garden City, down south. But they move to New Brighton, over the water, as he gets a job there and they don't like it one little bit. In fact they have both run away and as soon as the older one, Satu, makes enough money playing her music, they will be straight on the train at Lime Street, back to Letchworth, no messing.

Nocker says, "Come on, Scouseland's not too bad really. And you can always see Everton at home." But she just tells him she don't know any Mr. Everton, nor where his home is. Then she starts crying and saying she misses her friend Lizzie.

We are doing our best to cheer her up when this voice comes from behind us: "Now then, what's going on?"

We turn round and see a lady scuffer, not any old lady scuffer neither but none other than WPC Coplady, what used to be our teacher one time till she has a nark with Basher and goes back to the force and is very, very tough indeed.

She starts asking all questions about what two nice little girls are doing with a pair of roughnecks like us. I give Satu a nudge not to say anything, so then she begins talking to Sanna the little one.

She says, "Be a good girl and tell me what your name is, or the fairies won't love you," and suchlike crap. Sanna takes her lollipop out of her gob and says back that the fairies *do* love her, as they give her ten pee for her tooth only last week.

WPC Coplady says, "How sweet," and bends down to pat her on the head. Next thing this little judy nuts the female busy in her belly button so hard that she flops down on the seat of her fat keks going, "Oof, cor, Woof!"

Me and Nocker grab hold of one little judy each and take off immediate. We hear a train coming into the station so we belt down to the platform and hop on it before the doors close. The train starts off, but after a hundred yards it stops again and don't move for quite a while, which is typical.

I ask Sanna why she nuts the scuffer judy and Sanna tells me it is because she doesn't like her face. Then she whips her book out and says she is going to read to us. Neither of us are keen about this, as the book is called Pippy Longstocking and looks real wet, but we don't like to say no to somebody what can k.o. WPC Coplady, no bother. So she starts off and she don't read bad at all, in fact a whole lot better than most of the lads in our class.

After a bit, while we are listening, she drops her ball and it makes a sound like 'Clang.' She picks it up and says it is a rotten ball as it is made of iron and she finds it in a flower bed at the festival. It has also got this ring thing at the top which gets in the way, so she is going to pull it out now, which she does, immediate.

Next thing, the ring comes off in her hand, a kind of handle at the side comes up and there is a fizzing noise. We both catch on straightaway to what has happened, which is that this little judy has got hold of a World War 2 hand grenade, what has been left over from the tip that they build the Garden Festival on.

Nocker can act real fast when he thinks his earhole is going to be blown off next second. He grabs hold of the thing and cobs it out of the window. Then there is one almighty bang and the whole carriage shakes like a jelly. The train starts up immediate but it goes back to the station we just leave and all the doors open again.

The people rush out on to the platform saying, "What's going on, flaming Mersey Rail again, it needs a bomb under it!" which they don't realise just happens.

We gallop up the station steps but when we get to the top there is scuffers to the left of us, scuffers to the right of us and WPC Coplady behind us. There is only one way to run and that is back to the Garden Festival.

When we reach the turnstile we know it is the end of the road and we get ready to turn round and say, "Okay coppers, we'll come quietly," even though we know we will most likely get twelve years to life for blowing up a railway line. But next thing there is all flash bulbs going off and fellers like Billy Butler from BBC Radio Merseyside and the Granada Television man are shoving microphones under our gobs, as it seems that they have been waiting for the two millionth visitors to the Garden Festival and we are the lucky ones.

Nocker gives them an exclusive interview. He says it is a real honour to be picked like this and he is made up about it. He is not joking about this last bit neither, specially when he can see Basher, the ice cream man, the scuffer what Duff cobs on the helmet and the keep fit judies and fellers, all waiting to do us and who can't get near now because of the crush.

All they can do is follow us round and watch while we get the treatment, like rides on that steam train they have got there, and loads of smashing grub; the lot. We also get given a big fat cheque, while Satu plays her violin for the telly people and they buy Sanna a nice new ball.

The trouble is though, Merseyrail find out about the bomb on the line. They make us give the cheque back to pay for the damage we do, as the Hunts Cross-Kirby line is nackered for a long time. Mind you they don't say nothing about the blowing up, but just say the delay is due to staff sickness, and all the passengers say, "Another load of bloody drivers what can't turn in because they have got hangovers!" and go and queue at the bus stop.

But we have a bit of luck with Basher. He is so pleased about us being the two millionth visitors that he don't cause us no aggravation, as he reckons it has brung credit on his school.

Nocker comes looking for me a week or so later, to show me a letter what he gets from them two little judies over in New Brighton. He finds me in the public library, where I don't go very often, and I hope he doesn't find out that I am looking on the shelves for Pippy Longstocking, as I never did hear the end of it when Sanna reads it to me.

In the letter Satu says, "Thank you, you two nice boys, for looking after us." She also tells us that she don't think Merseyside is too bad now, as her school orchestra wins first prize at the Festival, also her friend Lizzie has come from Letchworth to stay with her for a bit.

At the end of the letter she asks Nocker how that nice Mr. Everton is, that Nocker was talking about, and could he send her his address, as she would like to pay him a visit at his home? Which just shows you that these Southerners have got a long way to go before they get as smart as us lot up here.

9

Nocker Yates and the Tourist Trade

"That Chancellor feller has give us something that money can't buy," says me Mam, after she sees what the Budget does to the prices of ale and fags. And when we ask her what, she says, "Poverty." Then she shoves her hat on and pushes off to spend ten quid at the Bingo, to help the housekeeping along.

Me and me best mate Nocker Yates suffer considerable as well, when we have to pay a lot more for our quiet ciggy. Also the Budget puts the mockers on the car-minding business real good, too. Each time we go up to some feller and say, "Keep an eye on the Rolls for you Mister, while youse is enjoying yourself in the alehouse with the lady," he tells us to shove off as the motor is going back to the hire purchase company tomorrer, he can't afford ale no more, and that is no lady that is his wife, and fat chance of anybody enjoying theirselves while she is around.

In fact it gets so bad Nocker calls me to a share-holder's meeting in the shed where his old feller keeps his pigeons.

"Things is getting real desperate," Nocker says, after he chucks something at a bird what divebombs his nut. "The way it is going we won't be able to afford a ticket at the Free Library soon. You got any ideas about how to raise the wind?"

I say how about trying to flog the picture what is hanging in his outside lavvy. This is a genuine P. Picasso painting and Nocker gets hold of it when he is taking his own drawing to Rembrandt, the screwy art teacher at our school. He bumps into this feller outside the Art Gallery, both of them drop what they are carrying, and each pick up the wrong parcel. In the end Nocker's picture gets hung in the gallery with a lovely gold frame round it, and his old lady puts the real P. Picasso in their bog, so her mates can look at it sitting down in comfort, as she thinks her baby boy done it all by himself.

"No chance," Nocker says back. "Last time we try that lark we get chased by half the scuffers in Liverpool, I end up in an Egyptian mummy's coffin and Basher gives us the stick. Anyhow the old feller puts his foot through it last week. He says that looking at a judy with

51

two eyes one side of her face and three you-know-what's will put him off it for life, if he isn't careful."

We keep nattering on like this for a bit and getting nowhere. Then Nocker gets cheesed and says the meeting is closed.

"No use sitting here like spare parts at a wedding," he tells me, "we have got to go where the action is. So we make for town and see what we can pick up."

I ask him how we are going to get there, seeing as how we are so broke we can't even afford the five pee bus fare.

"We walk," he tells me, "there isn't no other way." And now I know that things are proper bad, as Nocker don't consider walking to the lavvy even, if there's a chance of a taxi.

Anyhow we start off to hoof it all the way to Church Street. Nocker tries to hitch a lift in Scottie Road but nobody stops for us. In the end we get so nackered we just have to sit down and rest, so we park our bums on the edge of the kerb in a back crack, somewhere between Victoria Street and Whitechapel.

This is a real scruffy sort of dump, with more pepsi cans and chip papers than usual lying about. There is a caff over the road from where we are sitting which is called the Armadillo or something. A lot of fellers keep coming in and out of it carrying guitars, with long hair and nitty whiskers and they all look like a good wash and brush up wouldn't do them no harm.

Then all of a sudden a coach comes round the corner and parks so near to us it almost chops our legs off. A lot of young fellers and judies climb out. These are all dressed real posh and have got cameras slung round them.

Next thing one of them points to the name of the road and starts jabbering to the others in some foreign lingo. When Nocker sees what's going on, he nudges me so hard I fall off the kerb.

"Come on," he says, "this is where we move in."

I ask him what it's all about. "The tourist trade, that's what it's all about," he says back. "Them lot have come all the way from foreign to see our beautiful city and it's our job to show it to them, at a price of course."

I say, who is going to want to be shown around by a couple of scruffbags in parkas and school keks, but Nocker says not to worry. Anybody what comes to Liverpool for their holidays is bound to be screwy and an easy touch. And when I want to know how we are going to talk foreign he says he will manage the chatting up part, no bother.

Next thing, he goes up to the fellers and judies and bows to them, like he is flogging Japanese cars on the telly.

"Ah so," he says, "Good night please. You speak English, yes?"

They all stop their snapping and jabbering and turn to look at him, like he escapes from the zoo. Then one of the judies, a real smart tart, comes up to him.

"Excuse me," she says, "but I am not understanding quite what you say. Do you speak English by any chance?"

Nocker is narked at this and says back of course he understands English, real good. The judy don't understand this neither and Nocker gets a bigger cob on. In the end though they manage to get across to each other.

She tells him she is called Gudrun and comes from Hamburg in Germany, so do all the rest with her. It seems they are mad about the Beatles and want to see their home town. Nocker says back we both belong to Scousetours Limited and will show them round for very reasonable, cash only, no cheques and no soap powder coupons.

Gudrun says OK and she is hiring us as guides, that is if we are members of the English Tourist Board. Nocker don't get this, but he tells her that we are and also we can accept school vouchers. He sees this last bit wrote up in a shop somewhere and thinks it is a good line.

Then he asks them where they would like to go and recommends Everton footie ground as one of the best sights in Liverpool. But Gudrun says they want to see the Cavern first, which is a place where the Beatles used to sing and play guitars one time. We are in trouble straight off, as we don't know nothing about classical music being strictly Heavy Metal ourselves. Just as we are scratching our heads and thinking what to do, one of the tarts says she wants to go to Penny Lane.

Nocker gets the wrong end of the stick immediate. He says there is a public lavvy in the next street but it is strictly Gents only. Gudrun tells him that Penny Lane is a road what the Beatles make up a song about and she starts looking at him a bit odd like. Nocker says, "Of course, of course, what am I thinking about? Everybody get on the bus and we'll take youse there."

While they are all piling on the coach I grab Nocker and ask him if he knows what he's doing. He says he hasn't got a clue, but we'll just have to box clever and it'll turn out all right.

The bus driver starts off and straightaway there is trouble as he is foreign too. It seems they drive the wrong side of the road where he comes from. He thinks he is still back home and nearly flattens two fellers before he remembers what he is doing. These shout bad words after us. Gudrun asks Nocker what they are saying, as she is always trying to learn more English, which is most embarrassing all round.

Nocker gets by the driver and keeps telling him things, like, "Turn right, go left here, straight on there, watch that old lady with the shopping trolley," and so on, as if he really knows what he's on about. This is all right for a bit, until the fellers and judies get restless and start asking questions and wanting to know when we are getting there. I say to Nocker he'd better do something quick, or we are in dead lumber. I also tell him we keep going round in circles as we pass the same scuffer on point duty five times already. He says back to belt up as he wants to think.

Then the tart what said she's like to see Penny Lane finds out she has got to go to the lavvy for real. Nocker sees a public bog and tells the driver to pull over by it. The judy hops off and all the fellers make up their minds they are caught short too so *they* pile off and follow her. The trouble is they go after her down the same steps as it seems there is no difference between the Ladies and the Gents where they come from.

Next thing there is a whole lot of hollering and screeching and they all come back up like the clappers with the lavatory lady chasing them and waving her bog brush ready to give them a clout with it.

They get back on the bus and start giving us dirty looks, like it is all our fault. Nocker tells the driver to shove off quick, as he don't like the look of that bog lady one little bit. Also he reckons it will be harder for the tarts and fellers to grab hold of us and do us if the bus is going quick, as they are starting to moan and complain considerable.

Nocker is real stuck for a way to get us out of this mess what we are in. Just then he sees a supermarket across the street and he has an idea. He shouts the driver to stop, which the feller does so quick he sends everyone flying which don't improve matters. Gudrun wants to know what's up and Nocker points to the name of the store, which is called Lennon's.

He tells them that this shop is owned by the auntie of one of the Beatles, John Lennon. He also says that tourists from foreign can get everything half price there. He is hoping that they will all dive in immediate and we can make a getaway in the rush.

All of them are made up about this, except the Gudrun judy. She pushes off up the road and goes into a phone box for some reason or other. Also the rest of them grab hold of us, before we can do a crafty slide-off and say we have got to show them round the shop. So it looks like we are right in it.

Anyway they all go round with their trolleys and load them up with all kinds of stuff, booze, fags, the lot. When they get to the place where you pay though, the check-out lady says she don't know about things being half-price, nor about any John Lennon's auntie and if they don't pay up what the till is showing she is calling the scuffers.

Just then Gudrun comes back from the phone box. She says she has been ringing up the English Tourist Board who tell her they never hear of Scousetours Limited before and don't want to hear now.

Things start to look serious. All the lot of them begin giving us the eye, like they want to work us over and the fellers, who are very big and muscle-bound roll their sleeves up. Nocker gives me the word to split and we take off like the clappers.

They come on after us and trouble is they can all run real fast. Very soon we are out of puff and it looks like we are going to get a battering. Then Nocker spots the supermarket trolleys what are all left outside the place.

"Come on Scouse!" he shouts me and he jumps on one of these and shoots off down the hill, which is very steep.

I grab hold of another trolley and follow him. We start going faster and faster and can't stop. Then we get to the traffic lights at the bottom which are on red. So Nocker does a crafty swerve as he sees this lorry which is coming right across his path. Next thing his trolley bashes into the kerbside and he goes flying through the bedroom window of a bungalow which is dead opposite.

He lands on the bed in this place, next to some young judy what is fast·asleep. She wakes up smartish though the minute Nocker appears and just then her old feller comes in through the bedroom door. He arrives home unexpected as he is on day shift at Fords and they are out on strike again, sudden. Naturally he wants to know what Nocker is doing next to his Missus in bed and Nocker is having a lot of trouble explaining. For once in his life he is glad to see the scuffers, who turn up to sort things out after the supermarket lady calls them.

They have us in Juvenile Court next day. We get done for nicking a supermarket trolley, exceeding the speed limit on this, going through a red light on it and also being in charge of same without displaying

L-plates and without having a qualified driver alongside. One of the magistrates, who is a judy, wants to throw in something about Scousetours Limited as well and charge us with false pretences, but my old lady who is there too says out loud that she has got a nerve, seeing as how the inflatable bra what this judy is wearing is false pretences enough for anyone. So in the end we just get probation and told never to do it no more.

Nocker is real cheesed about all this. And he is more cheesed when he gets a letter from Germany, addressed to Scousetours Limited. This is from one of the judies what we show round, who don't speak English so good and don't really catch on to what happens at the supermarket. She says she leaves all the stuff what she buys, behind in the shop, and will Nocker kindly settle up with Lennons and post it on to her and next time she comes on one of our wonderful guided tours she will pay him. But, as Nocker says, anybody what comes to a dump like the Pool for their holidays is bound to be a bit of a divvy.

10

Nocker Yates Studies his Environment

"If ignorance is bliss," says me Mam, when she takes a look at the school report what I bring home, "youse must be the happiest divvy on the face of this earth." Then, after she gives me a few good belts across the lughole, she puts her hat on and pushes off to have a word with Basher our beloved headmaster, about getting some knowledge knocked into me thick head for a change. At the end of the street she bumps into Ma Yates, the old lady of me best mate Nocker, who is likewise wanting her blue-eyed baby boy learned a bit better than previous.

Basher is in his office when they get there, nattering to some long skinny puff with nitty whiskers. He jumps to his feet with his hands at the ready, soon as they come busting in, as he meets them before and knows they are big trouble. But after he finds out they are not up on the bounce for once, he forgets all about Lesson One of 'Learn Yourself Karate', what he buys with money he nicks from the school fund and asks them real polite to park their bums. Then he shoves the seat of his own fat keks back in the headmaster's chair and wants to know what's on their tiny minds.

They both start telling him, loud-and clear, that they are cheesed to the back of their false teeth always seeing nought out of ten on our school reports and what is he going to do about it? Basher says back he will give us extra homework; also a few chops with his stick now and then so as we don't fall asleep on the job. Our old ladies think this is a cracker idea and can he start immediate, if not sooner.

But the feller what is with Basher begins shaking his head when he hears this and going, "Tut, tut, tut!" like he is watching Everton getting beat six-nothing by the Blind School, or perhaps even Tranmere Rovers.

"Really, Headmaster," he says, sounding as though he has got a hot potato in his gob. "That is not the answer to these boys' problems. What they really need is to be allowed to experiment with their environments."

My old lady says, "No way!" as I start doing this when I am in me pram and she has to batter ninety-seven varieties of nappy rash out of me to get me to stop. Ma Yates tells him likewise she is not having no more dirty things learned to her baby boy at school, not since he gets given sex lessons last year and she has to sew him up for the winter in June months ahead of schedule, just to keep him pure.

Next thing the feller is laughing his head off when he hears this and he makes a noise like our outside lavvy after you pull the chain, what the corpy won't do nothing about.

"Dear ladies," he says, "you are labouring under some form of mis-apprehension. What I am referring to actually is a totally new concept in education, pioneered by myself at that ancient seat of learning where I have a chair . . . "

Our old ladies have lost him after the first two words, so they look at Basher to see if *he* knows what the queer feller is chunnering on about. Basher tells them, quiet-like, that this is some professor from Oxford and Cambridge way, what thinks he has got hold of a new way of learning the lads. Meantime, the Prof. is galloping along like a runaway lorry full of encyclopaedias.

". . . The aim shall be a substantial improvement in the pupil's numeracy and literacy, thus adequately equipping him for adult life. This will be achieved, not by the traditional passive classroom rote learning situation, but by an active and stimulating exploration of the environment that surrounds his alma mater . . ."

Basher puts this in English too. He says with a bit of luck the Prof. might get us to count up to ten on our fingers one day, also we should know the right place to put our thumb-print for the dole money after we leave school. All this is going to be got done by letting us mess about in the street, instead of messing in class.

But he don't sound too gone on the idea himself, as he knows things can happen when me and Nocker get let out on our own. Perhaps somebody tells him about the time we get took to Chester Zoo with the Mixed Infants, and bring home this gorilla called Kong. Also he could be thinking back personal to when he takes us to Paris himself, with Mrs. Basher. Not only does Nocker get his nut jammed down a French lavvo pan, which is not nice, but Basher bumps into some tart called Fifi, what he meets first when he is there during the war; and naturally Mrs. Basher wants to know all about it. So nowadays he'd sooner keep us chained to our desks and have machine guns pointing down from the playground walls like them Jerry POW camps, if he could get away with it.

Our old ladies don't go much on us running round the streets neither, as they know we've been doing this for years and don't learn nothing except a load of bad language. But all the big words what the Prof. uses have give them a headache, so they say, "O.K., give it a bash, why not?" Then they push off home for a cup of tea and a laydown as they feel like somebody belted them over the nut with a dictionary.

Pretty soon me and Nocker get to hearing about this environmental malarkey and we start wondering whether it can be any worser than extra homework and Basher's stick. But, when the Prof. shows at the school next term we are made up as he brings a whole load of students along to help him get the show on the road. Not only are these studies judies, but none of their faces would stop a clock and they all go in and out in the right places.

Basher gets the lads together in the school hall to meet them.

"Now boys," he says. "Pay attention real good, or there'll be trouble. This here is Professor Winterbottom what has kindly come along to try and learn you something. He is a well-known expert on education, but that don't mean you can start your messing with him, you'll be sorry you was ever born if I get to hear of it. I will now hand you over to the Professor for a briefing."

Duff Riley, who has been giving the judies the once-over, says a spot of de-briefing is more up his street as far as they are concerned. Basher hears this and says, "Come out immediate, the boy what said that disgusting thing - or else!"

Duff sees Basher looking his way, so he points straight at Nocker who is standing next to him. This is because he wants to keep out of trouble, also he is narked about Nocker parking some stale chewy on his chair in class yesterday. So Nocker gets a battering from our beloved headmaster, who don't listen to a word about him being innocent.

Then Basher says, "I will have to leave you now boys, as I am very busy," and pushes off to his office for a quiet ciggy and a read of all the Beano's what he confiscates off of us.

Soon as he goes the Prof. starts splitting us up between the judies, two each. Me and Nocker get a right little blonde raver with all the fixings, who has already got tears in her eyes about the brutal way he just gets treated.

"You poor boy," she says to him, "Oh you poor, poor deprived boy."

Nocker don't go much on being spoke to like he was some brass monkey what gets locked in the fridge. But before he can say nothing she grabs him, sudden-like, and hugs him so hard his snitch gets jammed down the top of her blouse. Next thing he gets to realising he is a growing lad and there are more things to life than watching Everton win away and shoving chewy on Duff Riley's seat; as this judy, what is called Miss Bustington, sticks out so far in front she makes Raquel Welch look flat-chested.

Then she lets him go again and wants to know where he gets his shoes from. Nocker tells her in town, shopping with his Mam and she looks real surprised. It seems this is because she comes from down South, where they think everybody in the 'Pool goes around in their bare feet, when they're not nutting you in the bonce and saying, "Gizza job!"

All of a sudden, the Prof. is shouting us to gather round him again. He starts handing out a load of gear, like cameras and tape recorders and CB radios, also some big bits of paper and black crayons. He says all this stuff is to study our environment with.

When Duff Riley tells the Prof. he don't know what he is on about, the Prof. says back we are to go out with the judies and take photo's of the most beautifullest buildings we can find, like St. George's Hall and suchlike. We can also talk about them into the tape recorders and get through back to him on the wireless sets if we get stuck about anything.

Nocker wants to ask what the bits of paper and crayons is for, but there is so much racket by now, what with the lads going, "Testing, testing, testing . . ." into the radios and telling the judies to say, 'Cheese,' and snapping them with the cameras, that the Prof. can't hardly hear himself think. So he gives us a wave of his hand for us to push off, and we all go belting down the stairs like the clappers and into the street, with the judies following on behind.

Me, Nocker and Miss Bustington start walking up Scottie Road. After a bit she begins asking where all the beautiful buildings are, as she keeps looking round for them but can't see nothing. Nocker says this is probably because the Germans knock some down in the bombing and the Corpy sees the rest off with the demolition. Then she wants to know if it is far to St. George's Hall and suchlike, and can we get a bus there. Nocker tells her back that it is miles yet and all the buses are out on strike again. But, if she likes, he will take her to a building that will make St. George's Hall and all them buildings look like crap. She says, "O.K., so long as it's near," as her feet are starting to hurt.

So we do an about-turn and begin going back, along Great Homer Street this time. I ask Nocker where he thinks he's taking us, as the nicest looking place what I know of in these parts is the Gent's lavvy in Westminster Road, and *that* is nothing to write home about. Nocker says, "Everton's footie ground, where else?" and if I know anywhere better he'd like to hear of it. I tell him he's wasting his time as the judy is from down South, where they don't know about football as they only have bum teams like Chelsea and Arsenal. But Nocker says back she will be so made up she'll most like give him another one of them hugs, which is much better than any cheap thrill he can get from having a free read in the dirty book shop behind Cazneau Street.

So we keep hoofing it along Greatie, but by the time we get to the traffic lights at the far end, Miss Bustington is nackered real good. She sits down at the edge of the pavement and says she can't go no further unless we get a taxi or something. Nocker tells her there won't be no taxis round here till the alehouses start chucking out, and they come along to take home the fellers what are too bevvied to walk; unless he can get hold of a radio cab on the CB wireless set what the Prof's given him.

He turns it on, but all he can get is Duff Riley's voice. Duff has left his set switched on by mistake in the pocket of his keks, and don't know about it. Nocker can hear every word he says, when he is trying to chat up his studie judy, asking her what she is doing tonight and suchlike. So Nocker has to tell Miss Bustington, no way can he raise a taxi. She says it don't matter, as she leaves her handbag on the staff-room table in school and couldn't pay for it anyhow.

But then she starts to look real cheesed. Me and Nocker ask her, "What's up?" and she says she will be landed right in it if she can't come back to the Prof. with photo's of beautiful buildings, as this malarkey what we are on is some kind of test for the studie judies and she is going to get nought out of ten, by the looks of things.

Then Nocker wants to know if we can't do something with the paper and wax crayons what we are still lugging about with us. Miss Bustington cheers up immediate at this. She tells us that the Prof. is dead keen on something what he calls 'wax rubbing'. It seems you get the paper, shove it over a coalhole cover and draw on it with the crayon. This makes a sort of pattern and helps you to read and write real good, though how it does it the judy hasn't got a clue, as nobody tells her.

So we start looking for coalhole covers. But the only thing we can find anything like one is a sort of grid thing, what goes over the manhole where they put the telephone wires. What we don't know though, is that Duff Riley has been there already and done a picture of it. Just after, some British Telecom fellers come along and take the cover off to mend the wires what are on the blink. This nackers them so much they have to go off for a brew-up.

Meantime Duff, who is still hanging about, sees me and Nocker coming so he sneaks up and shoves his bit of paper over the hole, as he is still narked about the chewy Nocker put on his chair, hoping that Nocker will stand on the paper and fall in the hole, as his pattern looks just like the real thing.

Nocker does this; in fact he goes down so hard his grandchildren get shook up considerable. Duff is real made up and goes back to chatting up his studie a bit more. Next thing the Telecom fellers, who have finished their tea, reckon they'd done a good days work already so they come back and shove the grid back on. Nocker is now stuck in the dark and we don't know where he is as we are round the corner when it happens.

Nocker tries shouting for a bit, but nobody hears. Then he thinks he will try and get help on the radio. So he shoves up the aerial thing which gets stuck in the telephone wires, and no way can he pull it loose. Also when he switches on all he can get is Duff Riley again, still giving his judy the old razzmataz.

Just then Basher, who is in his room at school busy laughing his head off over Desperate Dan, hears the phone ring. He picks it up and some judy, who is one of the big cheese inspectors down at the Education Office, 14 Sir Thomas Street, comes on the line. She starts asking him how the Prof. is getting along with his environment thing, but before Basher can say anything back, all of a sudden Duff Riley's voice comes on the line. This is because the wire what Nocker's radio is stuck to leads straight to Basher's phone and is picking up Duff's voice.

Next thing the inspector tart hears Duff saying to his judy that he fancies her something rotten and can't live without her. He gets this way because his Mam feeds him loads of steak. But the inspector thinks it is Basher giving *her* the old heave-ho! She is made up real good about this, as she has got a face what would stop a clock, and the last time she was spoke to similar is during the war, when some Yank chats her up in the blackout by mistake.

So she says back to Basher, straightaway, "My darling, I didn't know you cared. I am coming to you immediate, my own true love," then she rings off and heads for the Education Office car park, as she reckons she won't have no more chances like this for a long time.

Meantime, back at school Basher is getting real worried. He don't understand what is going on, but he has the feeling that big trouble is heading his way. Also Mrs Basher will be showing up soon, bringing him his dinner, as he gives up eating school meals after they give him food poisoning. So he makes for the playground sharpish, as he thinks he might be able to send the inspector judy packing some way or other before she gets out of her car.

But this inspector is like all the big cheeses at the Education Office, nuttier than any fruit-cake on Kwik-Save's shelves as she don't have a motor car, but goes around on one of them three-wheel tricycle things. She comes belting through the playground gates on this and when she sees Basher standing there she makes straight for him, full of love and passion.

Next thing her front wheel knocks into half a brick what the lads use for a goal-post at playtime and she gets knocked for six. Not only does she go sailing through the air and land on Basher, but her frock gets stuck in the pedals as well and is ripped off of her. Then, who has to show up but Mrs. Basher carrying a bowl of hot scouse. When she sees her beloved one lying on the floor underneath a judy who is wearing nothing but a pair of comms. naturally she thinks he is up to his messing again, just like French Fifi in Paris. She is so narked she empties the scouse all over the both of them.

It all gets sorted out in the end with me and Nocker being blamed for everything, like usual. Basher has a cob on because he gets covered in scouse, the Prof. is narked on account of his environment malarkey blowing a fuse, the inspector judy goes off in a paddy after Basher tells her the big romance is all a mistake, and Miss Bustington is not very pleased when she finds somebody nicks her handbag what she leaves in the staff room. The scuffers come and question the lads about this, but they don't find nothing out. We reckon it was the teachers what do it anyhow, as they are always moaning about their lousy pay.

Anyway Basher says he is having nothing more to do with the Prof's screwy ideas. Then he stands over me and Nocker with his stick in his hand till we do three pages of English each, and what's more we have to get it all right before we can go home. He shows our work to the Prof. and says, "There you are, what did I tell you? My way is the only way with them deadbeats!"

So the Prof. goes back to Oxford and Cambridge and next thing, what do you know? We see him on telly talking about a new way of learning the lads, what he invents all by himself, which is giving everyone extra homework and a few chops of the stick now and again so as they don't fall asleep on the job. All the others on the programme, Robin Day and suchlike, think this is cracker and tell him he is a real smart feller. Basher is madder than a wet hen as he reckons the Prof. pinches his ideas, so me and Nocker get it in the neck from him - continual.

But, like me Mam says, "What you can't win on the swings, you lose on the roundabouts."

11

Nocker Yates – Pop Star

"If music be the food of love . . . " says me Mam each time the old feller comes back from the alehouse bevvied and sits playing his old Vera Lynn seventy-eights in his comms., with his false teeth on the mantelpiece, "then you'd better bring sandwiches." And, after what happens recent over the water in New Brighton, me and me best mate Nocker Yates couldn't agree more. It all starts when we get a letter sent to us.

"Dear Mr. Nocker (this says):-

Would you and your nice friend like to go to a concert next Tuesday at New Brighton bathing pool? My daddy can get us free tickets and you can both come to my house for tea as well before it starts if you like. Please ring this number tomorrow and let me know. I am at home all day as it is a school holiday.

Love and kisses – Satu.

P.S. Sanna sends love too.

P.P.S. I passed my violin exam with full marks.

Me and Nocker don't quite know what to do about this invite when we get it. At first we think we will just say, "Ta very much, but otherwise engaged," and leave it like that. Satu and Sanna are two very nice little judies. They have got them screwy names by the way, because their mam comes from Finland and is foreign. But for a start Satu, the big one, is always playing the Third Programme classical music stuff on that violin of hers what sounds like lovesick tomcats with gut-ache, so any concert she fancies is bound to be under the arm and no good. Her sister Sanna, the littlest one, is either wanting to read to you all the time from wet books like Pippy Longstocking; or she is nutting lady scuffers in the belly button and blowing up railway lines with old World War Two hand grenades, what she finds laying around on rubbish dumps. She does all this when we first meet up with them at the International Garden Festival, and me and Nocker nearly get landed right in it.

Then, after another think, we change our minds again and say, "Let's have a bash, why not?" For one thing it is getting harder and harder to duck in anywheres these days without paying, so even listening to a racket like pussycats with diarrhoea is better than nothing, if it is free; also the little judies' mam might come up with a real smashing tea. So next morning Nocker does a crafty sneak up to Basher's room for a free use of his blower, while our beloved headmaster is out at a meeting and the telephone monitor is having his quiet ciggy down at the bogs.

He manages to get through to Satu to tell her we can make it and he is real made up when she tells him we are not going to be lumbered with the classical crap after all, but that this is a pop concert being recorded special for Granada TV. All the big names like the Police, Frankie Goes to Hollywood and suchlike will be there and her old feller what is into show business as part of his job, can get us the best seats in the place.

Nocker says, "Ta very much luv for asking us, and what time do we come for our tea?" She lets him know that if we are on the train what gets to New Brighton station at a quarter to five they will meet us there. Nocker tells her back that quarter to five, New Brighton Station is fine as far as he is concerned. Then he says, "Tarra queen," and bangs the blower down. He heads for the door like the clappers in case our beloved headmaster comes back and catches him at it. In fact he busts into the corridor so quick, that he knocks somebody flying for six. This somebody turns out to be none other than Duff Riley, who is doing a spot of earwigging at the keyhole and hears everything what Nocker says.

Naturally, Nocker wants to know what Duff's game is. Duff says back that he knows all about the pop concert and he would like a couple of free tickets too, one for himself and one for his judy. Otherwise he will go and snitch to Basher about the way Nocker keeps using his room for a public telephone. And our beloved headmaster, he reckons, will do a lot more than just ask Nocker to put ten pee in the box provided to help along with the phone bill. He also lets slip that an invite to the tea party what Satu and Sanna are giving won't come amiss neither.

Nocker does not care one little bit for having the finger put on him by the likes of Riley, as them kind of things get right up his nose. So he lets Duff know, loud and clear, that the nearest to the free grub marlarkey Duff is likely to get if he goes snivelling to Basher will be a knuckle sandwich. Then he shoves off smartish as he sees through the corridor window that our beloved headmaster's car is turning into the playground; and also he hasn't had his own quiet ciggy down at the lavvy yet.

But Duff don't do no snitching though, not after he gets warned off, and me and Nocker are in the clear. Next Tuesday we make it downtown to Central Station, where you catch the New Brighton train. We are hanging around on the platform waiting for this to come in when we happen to notice a right pair of weirdo's standing next to us. This is a feller and a judy what are all dressed up in punk clothes and have got green and orange hair and a beard, that is the feller has got the nitty whiskers, not the tart. Then the train shows up and these get into a different carriage to us, so we forget all about them. We pass the time till we get there looking out of the window and writing EVERTON IS ACE all over the seats — in blue felt tip.

Nobody chucks an old pram or suchlike on the live rail for once, so we get to New Brighton only a quarter of an hour late, which is very good time for Merseyrail. There is the usual nark at the barrier with the ticket collector, with us saying, "Let us through Mister, we lost our tickets, honest," and him saying back, "Pull the other one son, it's got bells on, you Liverpool lot are all the same, trying to bum a free ride." In the end though he has to let us go, after telling us to push off quick before he batters us. We do as he asks and when we get outside the station, there are Satu and Sanna with a lady what is their mam waiting for us, so we go over to them.

Both the little judies say how pleased they are to see us and kiss us all over our gobs — which is most embarrasing. In fact we are glad nobody is around to watch this, except the two punk weirdo's what have shown up again sudden like, and are standing right near us, looking all round them like they don't know which way to go next. I notice that the feller is giving me the eye sideways, as though he knows me from somewhere else, and I also get the feeling that I see him before.

Then the little judies introduce us to their mam. She don't kiss us, thank goodness, but just says she is sorry her old feller can't be there too to welcome us as he is busy down the Bathing Pool, getting things ready for tonight's show. After that she tells us to come along to have our tea.

While we are going along the road on the way to their house, I happen to turn round once and I see that the two weirdo's are walking behind, like they are following us. But then we turn a corner and I don't see them no more and in a few minutes we get to where the little judies live.

We go inside and their mam says to them to take us in the front room and look after us while she gets cracking with the tea. They are doing just this, with Satu telling us all about her violin exam, while Sanna reads to us a bit more from Pippy Longstocking, when the front door bell goes "Dink, donk, dink, donk" all of a sudden. The mam shouts to see who that is as she can't go herself, being too busy. Satu goes off to answer the bell, and we hear her nattering to somebody or other in the hall for a bit. Then she comes back and we see that she has brung two people with her. These two are the weirdo's what seem to keep popping up all round us, ever since we left Central Station.

Satu tells us that the feller and the judy are the lead guitarist and vocalist from some pop group what is called 'Scouse-song.' They are doing a gig at the show tonight down at the pool, but they manage to lose their way as they don't know New Brighton too good. So they ring the little judies' old feller, who is still busy getting things ready, and has given them the bathing pool number, just in case. It seems he says to them to come up to his house, and then we can show them the way later. He also says that the weirdo's can have their tea with us.

Anyway they sit down and Satu, who knows quite a bit about pop music as well as the classical crap, starts asking them questions like, "How many times have you been on telly? Have you got on Top of the Pops yet? and who is Scouse-song anyway?" as she's never heard of them before, and suchlike. The feller don't say much to this except to grunt into his beard and the judy justs sits there. All the time this is going on, Nocker is looking hard at them both, like he knows them too.

Next thing their mam comes into the room lugging a whacking great tray what is loaded with all kinds of smashing grub. Soon as they see this, the weirdo's start licking their lips like they get nothing to eat but free school dinners for months. The mam hasn't time to plonk the tray on the table before they are at it. The feller grabs two sausage rolls and stuffs them into his gob, while the judy does likewise with a big cream cake. They both begin scoffing away, and their manners is worser than Riley's pig.

Then, just as they swallow the first lot down and stretch out their hands for more, Nocker jumps up to his feet.

"Youse is rumbled, Riley," he yells out and makes a snatch at the feller's hair and nitty whiskers. These both come off in his hand, and who do we see standing there, large as life and twice as horrible but Duff Riley himself, in person, what has been disguising himself up with a wig to gate-crash the teaparty, and also to duck in the pop concert after — for free!

Naturally I am most surprised at all this, and as for the little judies' mam, she is taken to the door good and proper. She starts asking, loud and clear, will somebody kindly let her know what the score is and just what the hell is going on in her own house? Duff says back it is only a joke, what he thinks he will play on Nocker who is a great mate of his. At this Nocker gives out to all concerned that he wouldn't touch Duff with a disinfected barge pole, not for all the Cup Final tickets in the world.

The mam gets a right cob on when she hears this and she tells Duff she will be most obliged if he would beggar off immediate and take his judy with him as well. Then Duff starts whining and begging, the way he does to Basher when he thinks he is going to get the stick.

He says, "Ah eh Missis, don't be tight, let's stop for our tea, we're starving." But she informs him that he had better move the seat of his fat keks at once, otherwise she is going to phone the scuffers to come and take him away in a plain van. So they have to split, after they let rip with a whole load of bad words; and we are real glad the little judies have been well brung up and the mam is foreign and none of them don't know what these mean.

Nocker sees them off of the premises to see that they don't try to nick nothing on the way out. As he is standing by the garden gate and watching them go down the road, just to make sure they don't come back and cob a half a brick through the window or something, it starts to come on to rain proper heavy. Duff gets narked at the thought of getting a soaking so he turns round and shouts back at Nocker how he is going to do him for this, some way or the other. Nocker don't take no notice as he knows Duff can't even punch his way out of a wet paper bag, and he turns back to go in the house and gets his tea.

This turns out to be a real smashing bit of nosh and we get stuck into it, no messing. Mind you, we don't act like Duff and his judy. We know this is a posh sort of place, where they tell the kids not to spill on the tablecloth before the old feller reads it, and you have to say "Pardon" each time you let off, so we remember our manners. After we finish, the mam goes into the kitchen again and washes up. Then she says it is time we shoved off to go to the concert.

When we get outside it is still hissing down cats and dogs. The little judies' mam apologises to us and says we have got to walk, as her old feller has took the car early on and all she can give us is some umbrellas. We start off with these over our nuts to keep us dry, and while we are going along a feller comes belting past in a big motor car. He goes through a puddle when he goes by Nocker and splashes him all up his keks. Nockers just stops himself shouting out how this driver's father wasn't married to his mother, in time.

Then we get to New Brighton Bathing Pool and find there are thousands of fellers and judies pushing and shoving to get in through the doors. There is also a load of scuffers shoving and pushing these back and telling them to get in line proper; and sometimes giving one or two of them a crafty belt across the nut with their truncheons when they think nobody is looking. But the mam don't go near this lot. She takes us round to a side door and shows some tickets to a man there and we are let in immediate.

As we are going along a passage way to where our seats are, she takes a look at Nocker and sees that his keks are sopping wet. She tells him he can't possibly sit in them all night as he will catch his death. So she finds a little room what has got a radiator in it and tells him to park his keks on this. After they are dry he is to come and find them where they are sitting in the very best seats in the place.

Nocker does as he is told. He's sitting there in his comms., watching his keks steaming away and thinking back to the times when he is in Mixed Infants and his short pants have to be put on the school radiator each time he wee's himself, when he hears a noise outside the window.

He goes and takes a look to see what is going on. And what does he spot but Duff Riley, turning up like a bad penny again, who has ditched his judy some place and is now shinning up the drainpipe to get into the concert.

Nocker shouts down and asks him what his game is. Naturally Duff don't expect no voices to come at him out of nowhere. The shock makes him let go. He slides down the pipe and hits the deck so hard with the seat of his you-know-what, it jars his grandchildren.

Nocker don't like Duff, who has worked some real dirty ones on him in his time. But he is soft-hearted and can't let him stay sitting there with his spare parts all shook up considerable. So he yells down again and asks Duff if he's all right. Duff don't answer, which makes Nocker think Duff must be hurt real bad. He explains to Duff what happens and that he hasn't got no keks on just now, but he will try and dial 999 or something to get help.

Duff still don't say nothing back, which makes Nocker think he must now be needing an ambulance, or something like that, urgent.

He gives Duff the wire about what happens to his keks, and hopes Duff will understand what a good skin he is to be rushing all over the place on his account without no trousers on. Then he pushes off to find somewhere to ring up.

He sneaks down the corridor looking for a blower and hoping no-one sees him, but he don't find none. In the end he goes through a door, as he thinks perhaps it will be an office what's empty and has a phone in it. He makes a real big mistake here though, as what he goes barging into is the changing room of the judies what are doing a dance routine at the pop concert. And what is more, the place is full of these same judies, all chucking their bra's and knick-knacks round the place and slopping make-up on their gobs. In fact, it reminds Nocker of the pictures what he sees in the dirty bookshop behind Cazneau Street, where the lads go for a free read and a cheap thrill, and he is most embarrassed.

But he is not one tenth as upset as what the judies are when they see him come barging in. They jump to the conclusion immediate that he is one of them sex maniacs they read about in the Liverpool Echo what go around without no clothes on and they start screaming and fainting all over the place. A couple of scuffers, who are having a quiet ciggy some place nearby where the sergeant can't see them hear the racket and come along to see what's up. The minute they clap eyes on Nocker they grab him, twist his arm up his back and tell him he is nicked.

It takes Nocker quite a bit of time to let these busies in on as to why he is wandering around the way he is. Of course they say back, "We don't believe one blind word of it son," like usual. But in the end they come back with Nocker to the room where he leaves his keks, to check his story out. The keks are still on the radiator, quite dry by now, so the scuffers tell him to put these on and make himself decent for a change. Then they go over to the window to see if Duff is there, and after they do this they turn back again to say, "Just like we thought, there isn't nobody down on that pavement, what do youse think youse is playing at?" But they find they are talking to theirselves as Nocker remembers what his mam tells him at her knee when he is still firing volleys of crap into his nappies, which is to keep away from all scuffers, so he has already took off like the clappers.

He goes belting up the corridor again and the busies chase after him the way they are learned to do at the police college. After he turns the corner, he sees a big cupboard what they keep buckets and mops in and he dives into this to get out of the way. The coppers shoot right past as they don't see what he does, and everything goes all quiet again.

While he is waiting in there for the heat to cool off, he starts feeling like he wants to give himself a good scratch. He don't understand this, as it is far too early for him to get sewed up for the winter and he had a bath only last Wednesday week. What he don't know is that Duff Riley isn't really laid out cold when Nocker yells down at him from the window, before. He is just foxing, as he thinks if Nocker shoves off to get help he will climb up the drainpipe again and duck into the concert, with nobody to stop him this time.

Soon as he gets inside the room, he spots Nocker's keks on the radiator. This gives him the bright idea of sprinkling the inside of them with itching powder, as he carries stuff like that round all the time, being the sort what lets off stink bombs on the tops of buses and suchlike. Then he takes off to find himself a good seat so as he can watch the show.

Nocker stays inside the cupboard scratching away at his spare parts till he can't stand it no longer. He shoves open the door again, and he is so taken up with his personal problems that he don't take a blind bit of notice where he is going. Next thing, before he knows what he is doing, he finds he is standing on a kind of stage, in front of a whole lot of people all looking at him. There is also some fellers behind him, what have got guitars and drums and so on, and the minute Nocker shows up, these start belting it out with some heavy metal stuff.

It seems that this is a pop group what is waiting for their lead vocalist to turn up, as he is very late because he is still in the alehouse across the road having a bevvy and forgets what time it is. So when the band see Nocker they think there has been a change of programme and he has become part of the act instead.

But Nocker couldn't care less by this time, as the itch has got real bad. He tries to make it a bit betterer by twisting and turning all round the stage and waving his hands up and down and things like that. The crowd of fellers and judies in front of him don't know this though and they think he is doing some kind of a dance. They start to clap and cheer, as they have got proper cheesed waiting around for the action to begin.

Then Nocker, while he is poncing round the place, sees Duff in the front row, sitting next to a feller what has got glasses and a big cigar stuck in his gob. Soon as Duff finds Nocker looking his way he gives him the two finger sign with one hand, and takes the box of itching powder out of his pocket with the other. He holds this up to let Nocker read the label which Nocker does, and then he knows what Duff has been up to and he goes bananas.

He is so narked that he stands right at the front of the platform and points his finger down to where Riley is sitting.

"I'll f*****g get you Duff!" he yells out at the top of his voice, "I'll smash your face in Riley!" He keeps on shouting like this and wriggling and shaking with the itching powder which is getting real fierce.

What he don't know though is that he is standing next to a microphone which is switched on and the racket he is making goes all over New Brighton it is so loud. But the audience get sent good and proper and the fellers start jumping up and down while the judies are screaming and fainting and wetting theirselves, as it seems most pop stars point and yell and suchlike.

Next thing the two scuffers find out where Nocker has got to and they come belting on to the stage. Nocker spots them and packs in shouting. He tries to make a getaway and the scuffers begin chasing him round the place and in the end they grab hold of him and drag him off. Everybody thinks this is still part of the act and by now they are ripping up the seats and chucking these at each other, they are so made up with the show. As Nocker is being given the bum's rush off of the platform, he happens to see Duff Riley is chatting up the feller with the glasses and cigar, what is next to him.

This whole business takes a lot of time to sort out.

After they take Nocker away to the scuffer station and lock him up, as they think he's dangerous, they have to send for the little judies' mam to come and say who he is, after Nocker starts to get across to them what happens. Also his own old lady and old feller have to be got out of the bingo parlour and the alehouse, and brung over to New Brighton so as they can take him home, as by now the busies reckon that Nocker is a bit gone in the top storey and mustn't be let out by himself. This don't please Nocker's old feller one little bit as he only has nine pints up to now, so he keeps on battering Nocker all the way back to the Pool.

Anyway Nocker keeps his eye out for Duff next day at school so he can work him over good and proper for landing him in it last night. But Duff don't show up nohow as it seems he sat down on a whole load of stink bombs what he has got in his pocket, while he is getting a bus back home to Scottie Road. These all go off at once and the niff is something chronic. Also the stuff what the bombs are made from gets stuck to his skin, so he has to be took to the Royal Liverpool Hospital and kept in a ward by himself till the pong wears off. In fact, he stays in the hozzy for weeks, and they only throw him out after they catch him peeping through the windows of a bathroom while the nurse judies is having their showers.

The next thing that happens is that they put the pop concert from New Brighton Bathing Pool on Granada Telly. And what do you know? Who do we see when we watch it, but Nocker himself twisting and poncing and pointing his finger, also he is singing! But the words what come out of his gob aren't the ones he yells at Duff Riley, as they have some sort of machine at the studio that they use with all the big stars and it can turn the noise a donkey makes into something like Barry Manilow, and it can also change all the words.

They put Nocker through this and he comes out singing in a real fruity voice and they change all the bad words he chucks at Duff into, "I'm looking at you love, with passion rising highly," or some crap like that. The lads at school look at the programme as well and they start taking the mick out of Nocker, telling him he is a puff and suchlike. Nocker has five fights in one day, and he only wins two of them.

Also, to make things worser than ever we find out that the feller with the glasses and big cigar, what Duff was nattering to at the concert, is some big theatre agent. Duff tells him he is Nocker's manager and he will sign Nocker up with him for the big time. The feller hands over fifty quid on account, which Duff pockets, and he don't find out for a bit that Nocker is only a scruffy school kid with nits.

When he does though, he starts coming round to the house asking for his money back, as Duff gives him Nocker's address not his own, and Nocker's old feller gets a right cob on when this happens and batters Nocker again. But, like me Mam says, "That's show business."

12

Nocker Yates and the General

"Old soldiers never die," says me mam, "they just fade away."

Speaking personal I don't know what she's on about, seeing as how me and me best mate Nocker Yates only ever come across one proper old soldier in the whole of our life, and he don't show much signs of fading at all.

This all happens early one November morning when we are on our way up Lime Street to start our paper round. This is not our proper line of business really, as the car minding is what we usually do to make a bit on the side. You know the sort of thing.

"Fifty pee to look after the motor, Mister, while youse is in the alehouse with the lady, only make it a quid on account of inflation." We are doing real cracker at it too, and then Duff Riley, from our school, goes and puts the mockers on.

It seems him and Nocker meet up in Cazneau Street one fine day, while Nocker is taking a bucket of horse manure to his uncle's plot at Fazakerley. Duff starts getting personal about the way Nocker's shirt is hanging out through a hole in the seat of his keks. Nocker gets real upset at this as he is a very sensitive boy; so he stuffs Duff's head in the bucket a few times. Then big trouble starts all round.

First Nocker gets a battering off of his uncle for spilling the manure all over Duff's nut, as it seems horse-flop don't grow on trees no more these days. Next Duff has a cob on because he just invests in a blow-wave at the Unisex Salon so as he can make it with the judies, and now these don't want to know him for some reason. So he starts thinking of ways to get his own back on Nocker.

In the end he gets to following me and Nocker around when we are at the car-minding. Just as soon as we knock off for a quiet ciggy he sneaks up and sprays all the motors with paint, the cash customers go moaning to the busies and these come round and tell us to lay off or they will do us, as they think it's our fault. Naturally we go looking for Duff to work him over a bit, but we find that he is now in with the

Delly Mob from up Kirkdale way, and there is too many of these for me and Nocker to handle.

So that is why we are going up Lime Street at six o'clock of a dark November morning; feeling very cheesed because the buses are out on strike again, the paper shop is miles away in Liverpool 8 and it's cold enough to deprive a brass monkey.

Then, just as we are getting near that war memorial thing in front of St. George's Hall what they call the Cenotaph, Nocker stops suddenlike and grabs hold of me arm.

"Look!" he says.

I stop as well and take a look. But all I see is a feller with a bowler hat on, the sort the blocker men wear at Cammell Lairds shipyard to stop rivets falling on their nuts, and also a young judy who is perhaps seventeen years old, what are both standing in front of the Cenotaph.

Then the judy turns round and straightaway I see what Nocker is on about, for this tart is none other than Nocker's big sister Julie. Though what she is doing here this time of day I don't figure as she never gets up before twelve, not even to go and draw her dole money. But before I can say nothing, Nocker's big kid turns round, sees us standing there, and starts coming over to us.

"Excuse me," she says real polite when she gets close, "but could you tell great grandfather and me the way to Scotland Road?"

And this is where we get big surprise number two, as the judy turns out not to be Julie Yates after all, but somebody what looks as like her as two tins of peas on Kwik-Save's shelf, except she talks proper posh and don't plaster lippy all over her gob.

Next the feller in the blockerman's hat comes over too when he hears us talking. He is very smart and military looking, though he is knocking on a bit, and he is wearing a camel overcoat with a Remembrance Day poppy in the buttonhole. The young judy, who is not Nocker's big sister, introduces him as her great-grandfather General Fortescue-Simms and says her name is Samantha Fortescue-Simms. We say back, "Pleased to meet you, I'm sure." Then she asks us the way to Scottie Road again.

Nocker tells them it is not a nice sort of area at all if they are looking for a bed and breakfast place, and they had far better try the Adelphi Hotel which is up the road and is the place where all the posh people go, though he can't recommend it personal as he don't use it much himself. The old general says back that they are not looking for that sort of thing, actually, but thanks very much all the same old chap. He talks like he has got a bit of a hot potato in his gob, but there is a look about him that makes you feel you had better not try taking the mick. Anyhow we get to nattering a bit. After a while, when we have become a lot more friendlier, the General comes across all of a sudden with the reason why they want to visit Scottie Road, which me and Nocker are dying to know.

It seems the whole story starts in World War I, or the Great War as the general keeps on calling it. He is over in France fighting the Germans while this is going on, though he is not a general yet but only a second-lieutenant. Also he is not having a very good time of it neither, as he is in this trench with his men and the enemy are chucking the lot at them, the kitchen sink as well. Just as he is thinking it is time to tell everybody to do a retreat and get the hell out of it, some kind of bomb what he calls a whizz-bang lands next to him, and knocks him out cold.

When he comes round, he finds he is in a hospital bed with a nurse bending over him. What is more, he is most surprised to find that he knows this nurse. As a matter of fact he knows her very well, and keeps on asking her to marry him when they are both back in England. But she always says, "No, nothing doing."

Naturally he is most chuffed to see her again, and straightaway asks her again if she will marry him. But all she says back is, "Don't be silly," and starts asking personal questions about the last time he has his bowels open and suchlike. Then the general wants to know next if the men what he was with in the trench are all right, as he don't remember nothing after he flakes out. The nurse judy says she don't know, but he is not to worry his little head about things like that or he won't get better, so go to sleep like a good boy. After that she pushes off with an armful of bedpans.

But the general just can't lie quiet. He keeps thinking about his men and worrying if they are all right. So in the end he gets up and puts his clothes on, as he wants to go back to the trench and find out.

Just as he is doing a crafty sneak-off the nurse judy comes round the corner and spots him at it. She don't want to lose her patient as he has got shellshock real bad, as well as a big hole in the side of the nut; also the Matron, who is an old bat, will give it her in the neck if he hops it. So she starts to chase after him.

She can't catch up with him though, he goes so quick. She keeps yelling at him to stop, but he don't take no notice of her. On they go towards the front line, past the British big guns first, all going Boom, Bang, Boom, at the Jerries; and next they start hearing the Jerry guns going Bang, Boom, Bang, back. These get to slinging so much crap all over the place that, just as the nurse judy nearly catches him up, the general does a dirty great dive into the cellar of a ruined farmhouse, as he don't want the seat of his keks blown off, and the nurse judy dives in too, right behind him.

Here he finds some of his men and he is very made up about this. But he is not so chuffed to find half a dozen Jerry soldiers there as well, what have took his lads as prisoners. There is also an officer with a pistol what he points at the general and says, "Hock dee Handen," or something, which is Jerry for "Stick'em up." So all the British are standing around like spare parts at a wedding with both hands stuck up in the air and wondering what is going to happen to them.

Then, all of a sudden, another English soldier comes in, as he wants to get away from the shelling too. In fact he rushes in so violent he knocks the Jerry officer flying, and makes him drop his pistol. The general, who is right on the ball, makes a grab at it dead smart, saying to all the Jerries, "Hock dee Handen yourselves!" which they do like the clappers, not wishing to get shot up the earhole, or some suchlike place.

Next, the general tells his own men to take the Jerries away somewhere and lock them up good. After which he turns to the feller what knocks the Jerry officer for six and asks him his name, and what he is doing here.

The soldier says back he is called Private Higgins A.H. of the Liverpool Irish, and he is looking for a mate of his, what he thinks gets wounded proper bad. The general is real pleased at this, and says that Private Higgins must be a cracker soldier, one of the best. Then he tells him that he is just the sort to take good care of the nurse judy while he goes away to see what happens to the rest of his men. She begs him not to go, as she wants to get him back to hospital, but he takes no notice of her, and pushes off.

After he spends all night in some place he calls 'No-Mans' Land,' he manages to find all of his soldiers. These are mostly wounded, except one of them that is dead. He is stuck to some barbed wire, and the general only recognise him by a name disc he has got round his neck, as most of his face has been blown off.

The general gets all his men to some place where they can be looked after, then he goes back to the farmhouse. He finds that the nurse judy is still there, but there is no sign of Private Higgins A.H. The general wants to know what happens to him, and she says he went off to his regiment half an hour ago, as he couldn't wait no longer. Then she tells him he looks proper clapped out and he must go away to the hospital again straightaway.

She keeps on nursing him when they get there, and he keeps on asking her to marry him. But she always gives the same answer back, "No, don't be silly."

Then, sudden-like, a couple of weeks later on November 11th, the day the war ends, she changes her mind and says yes. So they get hitched immediate and, not very long after, they have a bouncing baby boy.

All through the years they are married, the general keeps on thinking about Private Higgins A.H., and what becomes of him. He wants to find out where he lives and have a natter about old times, also he would like to thank him proper for knocking that Jerry officer flying. But each time he mentions this, his wife shuts him up and don't want to know about it for some reason or other, though she won't tell him why.

And then time marches on, and it comes to last week when the general's old lady goes and kicks the bucket. Naturally he is most upset about this, and don't know which way to turn, so Samantha who is his favourite great grand-daughter moves in for a bit to look after him, and help tidy up in the house.

They are going over the things on the old lady's dressing table yesterday evening, when they come across a little box in a drawer what has got a piece of paper inside, with Albert Henry Higgins, 147 Scotland Road, Liverpool, wrote on it. Also they find a Liverpool Irish soldier's cap badge.

The general gets all excited when he sees this, though he don't know how they come to be there. He says he must catch the midnight train from London, where they live, and come to Liverpool to see if Private Higgins is still alive. He wants particular to get here for today, as it is the 11th of November, when the Great War ends, also the day the nurse judy says she will marry him. So that is how they come to end up right in front of the Cenotaph where we met them.

Naturally, I am most interest in this tale, and Nocker has got his gob wide open all the way through it, likewise. Then the General asks one more time if we can show them the way to Scotland Road, so as he can have a crack at looking for No. 147, and Private Higgins A.H.

Here, Nocker shakes his head very solemn-like. He says he happens to know Scottie Road real well, seeing as how he is born and brung up there most of his life. But, he tells the General, No. 147 isn't there any more as they pull it down to make room for the Mersey

Tunnel. Also he hears his Mam and Dad talk once about some old feller called Albert Henry Higgins what kicks the bucket years ago, and don't leave no family nor relations whatever.

The old general looks proper sad at this. "Ah well," he says, "Private Higgins and myself will never meet again, not in this life anyhow. But I can at least pay my respects to the memory of a very gallant soldier." Then, sudden-like, he marches over to the Cenotaph and stands in front of it, stiff and straight like a ramrod, and staring into nothing.

Everything goes very quiet. Samantha and Nocker look at him and don't move a muscle. As for me, whether it's somebody practising or only in me mind I don't know, but I seem to hear a bugle playing soft and low in the distance, and just for that moment time stops still.

Then the General snaps out of it. He takes one step backward, chucks up a real smart salute, and turns round to come back to us. While he is doing this, we hear one hell of a racket from around the corner.

The fellers what are making the hoo-ha are Duff Riley and the Delly Mob, none other. Next thing they come in sight, loaded down with cans of paint and suchlike, and it looks as if they are going to spray the Cenotaph all over, with LFC IS ACE and so on.

The General spots what they are up to, immediate. He lets out one almighty yell.

"You louts," he bawls at them, "stay away from that war memorial!"

The Mob stops short at this, but when they see it is only an old feller what is shouting them they start laughing their heads off. Then Duff Riley thinks he will have some fun. He comes up to the old man and makes to knock his blockerman's hat off. Me and Nocker start worrying, as things look like getting pretty ropy.

The next part we don't see too good, it happens so quick. All we know is the General does a little sideways step, and moves both arms and one leg. Then Duff is sitting down hard, on the seat of his keks looking most surprised indeed.

The rest of the Delly Mob move in after that, as they think they can work the old feller over with not too much trouble. But then they likewise start flying all over the place as the General gets cracking with his arm and leg routine, and nobody don't seem able to lay one finger on him. In a minute they've had enough. They shove off like the clappers, so fast they don't wait to pick up their paint cans.

Nocker is most impressed with all this. He asks the General if he has been doing the Kung-Fu stuff, but the General says back, "No," and he has been doing something called Jiu-jitsu which he learns in Japan many years ago.

Then he says, "Well, time to be off I suppose, no point in hanging around here now." He shakes hands with me and Nocker and thanks us most civil for telling him all about Private Higgins. Samantha says good-bye to us as well. After that they head across the road to catch the London train. The last we see of them is when they turn round and wave at us from the way-in to Lime Street station. Then we push off too, to get to our paper round, as it is now very late.

All the time we are walking along, I am thinking very hard about something. In the end I speak to Nocker as follows.

"Why," I ask him, "didn't you tell the old General that Albert Henry Higgins is your great grandmother's brother? He will be made up to find out you belong to the family of the brave soldier what saves his life."

"Listen Scouse," Nocker says back. "I kept me gob shut about all that for this reason. Speaking personal, I never met Albert Henry Higgins myself, as they plant him in Anfield Cemetery long before I am a twinkle in the old feller's eye. But it is a well-known fact in the Yates clan that he is a no-good drunken bum. Why, he even flogs all his medals so as he can go and have a bevvy in the alehouse, and gets himself killed by a tram when he is going home across Scottie Road on his hands and knees."

"Also," says Nocker, "there was a saying in our family that if you leave your jar of ale, or your judy, next to Albert Henry for longer than two minutes you was asking for it. You saw how much like that Samantha is to our Julie. That nurse gets left on her own all night in the farmhouse cellar with Private Higgins. It don't need them sex lessons what we've been having in 4D this term to tell you what happens. And the General mightn't be very chuffed at all if he finds out his favourite great-grand-daughter is second cousin or something like that, to the Yateses." Then Nocker belts up and starts moving real fast, as it is getting later and later.

I follow behind him, and as I go along I get to thinking about the General and Private Higgins A.H. and the Great War. Then, all kinds of pictures come into me mind that I really don't want to look at; smashed up guns with dead soldiers lying round them quiet and still, and broken, twisted barbed wire with the feller with half a face hanging there. All of a sudden I hear that bugle again, sounding proper sad and I start to choke a little bit and tears come in me eyes.

13

Nocker Yates's Christmas Eve

"Christmas comes but once a year," says me Mam, and she is usually right without even having to look at the calendar. And when it comes this year, me and Nocker finds that we have got a hang-up over presents. Everybody tells you it is more blessed to give than to receive, but they never get round to mentioning the expense that this can cause.

"Business is so bad," says Nocker, "that we have just got to make sacrifices. We will both give each other a present, and everybody else will have to go without."

The business to which he is referring to is the car-minding trade. The trouble is that everyone is so broke in the Pool these days that they don't want to hand over for having their motors looked after. And also the scuffers start coming round and asking questions when we begin marking the bad payers with spray paint, though it seems the banks can all do the same thing with red ink and get away with it every time. There just isn't no justice left in the world at all.

Anyhow we decide to pack the whole malarkey in till the heat is off. The only thing is that we have set our hearts on buying ourselves one of them big cassette recorder things, what they call a blaster, so as we can do some body-breaking to it. This is on sale at a junk shop near Great Homer Street and is a bargain, seeing that it is on offer for twenty quid only, and it is not even a knock-off, being picked up off of the pavement in Cazneau Street after falling out of the boot of a parked car — accidental like. The junk shop feller has told us he will keep it for us till five o'clock Christmas Eve, so as we can get hold of the money somehow or other. But come the morning of the twenty-fourth we are still short of the asking price, as we only have fifteen pounds sixty pee. Things is real desperate, so Nocker calls a meeting of the shareholders, in the shed where his old feller keeps all his pigeons.

"We've only got a few hours left to find the rest of the money," Nocker tells me, after he tells a pigeon to get lost and wipes the mess off of himself. "What are we going to do?"

In the end, after a lot of nattering, we make up our minds to do a spot of carol singing, even though Nocker is against this at first as he says we will have to wait for night time, as all carol singing is done in the dark. But when I say that it's easier to dodge what is coming when it is light, as we are bound to have a load of crap chucked at us with voices like ours, he says back, "O.K."

We go down to the shopping precinct in Church Street first, where the big Christmas tree is. The idea is to stand there looking like two poor lost boys what have got no father and no mother, and get cracking with the Jingle Bells stuff. But when we get there we find a lot of little judies in their school clothes, with a nun in charge, have pinched our pitch, and are singing their heads off. They have also got a notice saying they are collecting for starving Asia or something, which gets Nocker real mad as he says this is unfair competition. He gets even madder when he hears they can all sing in tune.

So next we go down a side street and strike up at the door of an alehouse, the idea being that any customer what comes out bevvied will give us something. But we have no luck here neither, because I start with Good King Wenceslas and Nocker thinks he will do We Three Kings of Orient Are. The alehouse feller comes out and says will we kindly push off as we are turning his beer sour.

After this we don't know what to do. Then, as we are passing a bus stop, a number 80 stops to let the passengers off. Nocker makes a dive for it and pays for both of us, so I have to follow him on. When we have sat ourselves down and the bus shoves off I ask him what the big idea is.

"Scouse," he tells me, "the game's no good in town. We have got to go where the big money is, like Mossley Hill which is where this bus goes to, and is very posh. We can clean up big there."

After a bit the bus stops by a big church, high up, and we get off. It is very quiet when we leave the main road, to look for somewhere to start singing and there are not many chip papers and Pepsi cans lying around. We go round a corner and next thing some feller bumps into us and nearly knocks us flying, he is in such a rush. Nocker says, "Watch it, Mister," but he don't say nothing back, and then he pushes off like the clappers. Me and Nocker carry on walking, and before we go five steps we see a little old judy with white hair come out of her front door, all of a doodah. Before she knows where she is she slips on the garden path, and falls on her you-know-what.

We open the gate and go to help her up. I can see Nocker has got the same idea as me, which is that this could be a very rich old judy, who will remember us in her will when she kicks the bucket and we shall be able to retire before we leave school.

"Oh dear, oh dear," says the little white-haired old judy, when we get her on her feet. "You boys haven't seen a man from the Gas Board as you were coming along, have you?"

Me and Nocker tell her back that the only feller what we see is somebody tall wearing jeans and a bomber jacket who nearly knocks us for six a minute ago, but he is probably in Manchester by now he is going so fast. Then the little old judy goes, "Oh dear, oh dear," again.

"He says that he has to come in and read the meter," she says, "and when I tell him it has been done yesterday, he takes no notice whatsoever. After he goes I find out that there is a tin missing, what I keep all my money in. He probably picks it up by mistake. There was fifteen pounds in it, all the money I have got left out of my pension after I pay the electricity. It was for my Christmas shopping. Whatever am I going to do?"

Me and Nocker give each other a look, as we see just what the game is with that phoney gas board feller. We also can see that this is no rich old judy at all, and we have been wasting our time. But we help her into the house all the same as we can't leave her on the garden path, seeing as how she is shook up considerable.

We take her into her front room which is very clean and smells real fresh, but it is not posh, not one little bit. There is no telly and not a lot of furniture, and what there is don't seem up to much. She sees us looking at her sideboard which has got brass handles, so she tells us that it belonged to her great-great-grandma two hundred years ago, and is called Chippendale, or something. We begin to feel real sorry for her having to make do with clapped-out second-hand stuff like that.

Then she starts to feel a bit better and asks us would we like to have a cup of tea. We don't like to take it from her really as she is so broke, but it's cold enough outside to deprive a brass monkey, also she is a nice old judy and we don't want to hurt her feelings by saying "No" so we say back, 'Ta very much Missus."

While she is out in the kitchen boiling the kettle we happen to notice a photo in a frame what is stuck on the sideboard. This shows a feller in uniform, with one of them World War Two caps on, that go from the front of your head to the back of it. When the little old judy comes back with a tray covered with tea things and suchlike, Nocker asks if that is her old feller. She says No, but it used to be her fiancé one time. Then after we have settled down to swig our tea she tells us this tale.

It seems she first meets up with him down South where she is living at the time with her Mam, near a Royal Air Force place called Biggin

Hill. The war had just started and he is busy flying Spitfires, which he shouldn't be doing really as he is far too old for the job, being over thirty-eight. But the little old judy says he thinks it is his duty to fight for England, so he signs up and gives the wrong age.

The old lady also tells us that her Mam, who is loaded and has got a big house with all the fixings, is proper narked when she gets engaged to this Air Force feller, as he has got no money at all and also comes from Liverpool which she don't think is very nice. So when they decide they will get married on his next leave, and take a house in the Pool, the mam says no way will she ever speak to her daughter again, nor will the rest of the family neither.

But the little old judy couldn't care a toss. She tells her Mam to get lost, and comes up to get the place ready for the wedding, which is the house we are now sitting in at this very moment. Then, two days before his leave begins, the Battle of Britain starts up and her boyfriend gets the chop flying his Spitfire, so she is now left all on her own.

She says the only job she can get to make both ends meet is in some little sweet shop, what don't pay her very much. The years roll by and she gets too old to work and has only got her pension to live on. She is also very lonely as all the neighbours round about are real toffee and don't speak on account of her having worked in a shop. She even tells us that we can come again for a chat, any time we are passing, which shows how hard up she must be for someone to talk to. We are amazed when we hear this because you can always get a bit of company in Scottie Road when you want it, and quite often when you don't.

After a bit Nocker finishes his tea and then he says he will slip out and have a look to see if he can find the Gas Board feller for her, by any chance. I give him a nudge and tell him, quiet-like, that he has got to be wasting his time, but he don't take any notice.

In about ten minutes he comes back with a tin in his hand which I see is the same as the feller chucks away, and he hands it to the old lady and says, "Is this it Missis?" She says back, "Yes," and starts looking inside it, which I know will do her not a blind bit of good at all.

But then she gives a little scream, and next thing she is fishing three five pound notes out of the tin. After that she starts kissing Nocker all over his gob and saying that he is a very good boy, and that she will never forget what he has done. I can see Nocker is real glad Duff Riley and the other lads aren't here to watch all this.

After this, we find out it is getting late and time we pushed off. So we say tarra to the little old judy and split. All the way to the bus stop I am thinking very hard, and I keep on doing this while we are riding into town. Just before we get to Nocker's stop I speak to him as follows.

"It's all very well you putting our fifteen quid back in the old judy's tin," I tell him, "but that was the money what we saved up for our Chrissy pressie. Now all we have got left is sixty pee, less expenses. What are we going to do?"

"I'll tell you what we are going to do," Nocker says back. "Soon as I get back to our house, I'm having a word with me Mam. Then, if she says OK, me, you and our Uncle Bert are going up to Mossley Hill first thing tomorrow in his coal cart, and ask the little old judy to our place for dinner. It's a crying shame that a sweet old lady like that, what has given her feller in the war for the likes of us, should have to spend Christmas without no turkey and no telly. So she is most welcome at the Yates's, if she'll come that is, and don't mind mixing with a bunch of hard-knocks and rough-necks. If you don't like it, you know what you can do."

"She'll come all right, Nocker," I say, "She'll come. And I like it Scouse, I like it!"

Then we are nearly at Nocker's stop so he gets up and goes to the bus doors. He starts dinging the bell like Christmas chimes, but he packs this in when the bus feller shouts him and hops off onto the pavement. He doesn't do what else the feller tells him though, as his mam might batter him for being dirty.

The bus starts off again with a jerk what nearly breaks me neck, also it has begun raining and me feet are freezing. But I am feeling nice and warm inside.

THE END

OTHER TITLES FROM

Countywise

Local History
Birkenhead Priory .... Jean McInniss
Birkenhead Park .... Jean McInniss
The Spire is Rising .... Dorothy Harden
The Search for Old Wirral .... David Randall
Neston and Parkgate .... Jeffrey Pearson
Scotland Road .... Terry Cooke
Helen Forrester Walk .... K. Rickard
Women at War .... Pat Ayres
Merseyside Moggies .... R.M. Lewis
Dream Palaces .... Harold Ackroyd
Forgotten Shores .... Maurice Hope
Cheshire Churches .... Roland W. Morant
Storm over the Mersey .... Beryl Wade
Memories of Heswall 1935 — 1985 .... Heswall W.E.A.
Pillowslips and Gasmasks .... Joan Boyce

Local Railway Titles
Seventeen Stations to Dingle .... John W. Gahan
The Line Beneath the Liners .... John W. Gahan
Steel Wheels to Deeside .... John W. Gahan
Seaport to Seaside .... John W. Gahan
Northern Rail Heritage .... K. Powell and G. Body
A Portrait of Wirral's Railways .... Roger Jermy

Local Shipping Titles
Sail on the Mersey .... Michael Stammers
Ghost Ships on the Mersey .... K.J. Williams
The Liners of Liverpool - *Part I* .... Derek Whale
The Liners of Liverpool - *Part II* .... Derek Whale
The Liners of Liverpool - *Part III* .... Derek Whale
Hands off the Titanic .... Monica O'Hara
Mr. Merch and other stories .... Ken Smith

Local Sport
The Liverpool Competition (Local Cricket) .... P.N. Walker
Lottie Dod .... Jeffrey Pearson

History with Humour
The One-Eyed City .... Rod Mackay
Hard Knocks .... Rod Mackay
The Binmen are coming .... Louis Graham

Natural History
Birdwatching in Cheshire .... Eric Hardy

Other Titles
Speak through the Earthquake, Wind & Fire .... Graham A. Fisher
It's Me, O Lord .... Members of Heswall Churches
Companion to the Flyde .... R.K. Davies
Country Walks on Merseyside - *Part I* .... David Parry
Country Walks on Merseyside - *Part II* .... David Parry
A-Z Cheshire Ghosts .... Muriel Armand